Deception

Also by DJ Cooper

<u>Dystopia Series</u>
Beginning of the End
Long Road
Revelations
Dark Days

<u>Nine Meals from Anarchy Series</u>
Sun's Fury

<u>Anthologies</u>
Winter in the Apocalypse

Also by N.A. Broadley

<u>Apocalypse Trail Series</u>
Trail of Misery
Valley of Reckoning
Shattered Horizons

<u>Anthologies</u>
Winter in the Apocalypse

Dammit Peckerhead

Deception

The Insurrection Trilogy
Book one

DJ Cooper   **NA Broadley**

Angryeaglepublishing.com

Cover design by Piper Leigh Creatives

Editing by WMH Cheryl [http://wmhcheryl.com]

Angryeaglepublishing.com

ISBN: 978-1-7326212-9-9
First Printed in 2020

Chapter One

Kael sat straight up, sweat beading on his forehead. Barely moving he shifted his gaze about the small shack orienting himself. A shiver engulfed his body from the vivid nightmare, his arms instinctively closed around his body in reaction. Eyes dark, he shook his head to try and erase the images from his dream.

It was a rare moment when he managed a deep sleep. The nightmares plagued him almost every night now and he couldn't sleep much more than a few hours at a time before they'd return. His pallet on the floor, a thin strip of blanket with dried up grasses and a few pine boughs under it didn't provide much padding from the hard plank floor of the one room shack that he called home.

His left hip sang with pain and he groaned as he pushed himself to a sitting position. The images from the dream still burned in his mind. It was only intensified by the thin stream of light that shown through the small sliver of a crack in the wall. The rickety shack was full of holes where the frigid air streamed in and robbed them of what little heat they had. He shook his head and mussed his shoulder length chestnut brown hair straight back out of his eyes in an attempt to quiet the nightmare.

He let out an exaggerated sigh to bring him back to reality; one he was unsure was any better than the dream. His stomach growled. He was hungry. But then

again, he was always hungry. He couldn't remember a time when he wasn't. And cold… he was cold.

Each day anger tore at him, anger so dark and thick he found it hard to control. He clamped his fists together to keep from losing his temper and lashing out at his surroundings. Some days it took all he had to keep from tearing the tiny shack apart board by board. How could the Elites expect a person to live like this? It was inhumane. A growl escaped and he swallowed hard, pushing his anger deep inside. It would do neither of them any good for him to wallow in it. They were born to this, fair or not it was their life.

His eyes shifted to the old potbellied stove that had adorned the small room for as long as he could remember. He looked inside and sighed; the fire had burnt low, leaving just a few glowing embers. Cold drafts crept in through the slatted walls, brushing their frigid tendrils across the bare skin of his arm causing him to shiver.

A soft whimper drew his eyes to his younger sister, Zyla. She lay on the other side of the stove; curled up on her own pallet; shivering, her slight body shook under the one thin blanket covering her. His heart ached at the sight of her shivering beneath the covers. He reached back, picked up his own blanket and walked over quietly, draping it across her. His eyes filled with an expression of sadness as he stood over her and gazed down on her tiny, thin frame. His heart ached to see her suffer.

His expression changed as he looked about the room, finally settling on his own pallet, the dried materials of his own sleeping space would offer a few moments of respite from the cold nipping at her. He lifted the covering and drew out some of the material, then began to break the thin twigs of the pine branches, tossing them onto the few embers still smoldering inside the stove. Once it caught, he closed the damper to keep the fire low and prolong the brief moments of warmth before the cold drafts crept back in and robbed them of its comfort.

He had to find food today. She was his

responsibility now and she was hungry. This thought plagued him, and the anger pulsed like fire through his body, tensing his shoulders. He sat angrily, mindlessly continuing to break off the small pieces of bedding, while gathering the energy to rise up. They were starving to death and he knew it. Just like their mother had; just like many of his friends and neighbors.

The upper status scores, or elites as they called them, controlled their food. They were never given enough to get through until the next rationing. Each ration period he desperately tried to make the food last but her small hollow eyes staring into the empty bowl after the few meager scraps were gone, was agonizing. He'd let her have seconds and the few days before the rationing were always the worst. They still had two days to go and he cursed himself for not taking less food each time. His expression shifted from anguish to anger while he thought about it, vowing to do it better next time. The fattened pigs, as he and his friends liked to call them in secret; those who sat in their warm, comfortable, and lavish homes while others struggled for the basic necessities, were cruel and enjoyed watching the suffering.

Kael vowed that one day he would find the strength to stand up against the Elites. He would make them suffer far beyond the extent of what he and others were suffering at their hands. One day he would make them pay for the harm they brought upon them. He didn't know how he'd do it or when, but he swore, he would.

"One day," he muttered and got up to fiddle with the damper on the stove.

The Grays is what they called them, he and others like him, were a class of people that carried a low Social Score. The color was the color of your position, ranging from the dingy color of gray to bright and cheerful yellows and white. But the top classes were shiny with silver and gold. The scores dictated their status and those below a ten were barely considered human. His score was a mere four points. This meant his food and other supplies would be limited to only the minimum and consisted of little more than scraps from those with a higher social score. It was not even enough to survive. The worst of it was that it was very unlikely that he or Zyla; or any that were in this class, could ever rise above their birthed status.

Everyone was born into a family score and it was tattooed on them as a baby to keep parents from trying to smuggle their children into upper score areas and selling them to adoptive parents. They were treated as though the social score was a genetic marker that could not be erased. Those born with the social score of a Gray rarely ever gained another status.

He could gain a few points by helping the citizens with higher social scores when not required or excelling at a job offered. It could make life more bearable, but never would he be spared the arena when it inevitably reached zero. That would be his future; it was the future of all the Grays. They really had no choice in the matter. The lack of food and rise of desperation would eventually lead to the loss of social points. The use of unauthorized heating materials as he had done today would cost him a point. They could only burn what they were given for heat; they said it was because of the air. After the war, contamination was everywhere, but that was many years ago. If they gathered what was left in the fields before browns had been there, they were branded a thief. This kind of unauthorized gathering was considered stealing and was an instant zero. Anyone who would steal was considered socially outcast and no longer allowed to gain a social score.

The arena was the fate of those who had lost all points. If he won in the arena, he'd be given a magnificent meal, a swift painless death, and Zyla would have supplies for the season. If he didn't win? Well? He sighed in defeat as he tossed the last stick of wood into the stove. Zyla would surely die. He'd been training in secret as his father warned him. Training for the day when he'd be sent to the arena… or escape this life. He dared not think it for fear someone might hear his thoughts but the only hope for them was escaping Rysa and the Social Score.

The rays of light were creeping higher on the horizon, there was no time for this kind of mind wandering. He grabbed his jacket and jammed an arm into the sleeve. He took one last glance towards Zyla before he made his way out into the frosty morning. His worn boots, still a little too big, crunched on the ice-covered grass as he made his way to the woods.

He looked down as he sullenly walked along looking at his feet. They were his father's boots. Grays were not allowed to keep the belongings of family when they died, these would go to the allotment center. His mother switched the boots when his father went to the arena. His own boots were too small, and his toes poked out the end of them. He walked silently remembering that day with each step, thanking his father for the new boots that only had small holes on the sides.

The woods held an eerie darkness, calling out to him to run into them and never come back. They were forbidden, a sacred place they said was the life's blood of the zone. If only he could hunt to feed Zyla. She needed to eat, and a little protein would give her some energy and strength. It had already been two days and he could see her weakening; she was malnourished and a day without food took a dangerous toll.

Hunting was prohibited; every square foot of the zone was portioned off. Some for gardens, other areas wooded for wildlife to replenish. The higher areas were the upper classes; these were large buildings of the old city, separate from the rest of the classes with a high wall surrounding it. Each class as it sank in rank was further away from the city. Its villages scattered across the landscape. Classes were never to venture into other class areas that were not their own unless they had a pass to do work, and no one was to ever enter the preserve; the wooded area that surrounded the outer edge of the zone. If he got caught in the preserve, it would surely mean his death. It was a chance he was willing to take; it was their only chance. Soon they would run into the woods and further; even into the badlands if that was what it took to keep her safe.

Their zone was established right after the war. Vast areas of the countryside were devastated wastelands with small pockets that were unaffected. These were called the zones. Not all zones were alike, and each ran independent of others across the land. He lived in a zone where the score was everything. His village in the zone was Rysa, one of the villages furthest out.

Social scores were only a test in the before and had something to do with the war, but afterwards it became the rule in his zone.

He'd never been to another zone and questioned if any really existed. Rumored to be better he yearned to find out.

The Honor Guard that occupied his neighborhood could be paid to keep their eyes closed to some things like foraging. That is… as long as the village women were paying the price; forced to satisfy their every whim, in exchange for not reporting the illegal activity. This thought curled his stomach in revulsion. Any woman in the village over fifteen was a prime target for these animals. There was very little any of the men could do to stop them. His own mother had been forced to be a whore after his father died in the arena. She was assigned to a particularly twisted and perverse Honor Guard captain before she too died from abuse and starvation.

He remembered her coming home battered and bruised from Captain Akakin. He vowed one day to avenge her and the others with his blood. Many times, he'd come close to launching an assault upon his turned back. But his mother wouldn't allow it, reminding him that he couldn't take chances like that for Zyla's sake. It angered him, and he hated all of the guards.

He often wondered when a soldier of the Honor Guard would take notice of Zyla. Now that she was one month shy of fifteen, it was almost the age where she would be seen as serviceable for their pleasures. Kael was nearly panicked over the thought of it. She was quite small and frail in stature, it gave him hope that they wouldn't realize her age; but he knew full well that Captain Akakin kept track of the young girls. He demanded first rights to all of those who would come of age. Last season, he'd been seen dragging one girl from her meager birthday celebration to collect these first rights. The anger boiled inside him once again, his fists clenched, and his pace quickened.

He stopped and listened, tilting his head and craning to look behind himself. Someone was coming and it sent him diving behind a bramble bush. He'd heard the footsteps just in time and hid quietly watching. His knees pressed against the muddy ground, the cold and wet penetrated his ragged pants and his heartbeat echoed in his ears so loud he feared the man could hear it; pounding wildly in his chest. Eyes closed he concentrated on his breathing to slow it down before his heaving breaths did give him away.

He watched through slit eyes while the Honor Guard soldier stood just a few feet away from him. Cigarette dangling from his lips, eyes gazing out over the desolate parking lot, now overgrown with weeds. Kael felt a surge of hatred, enough that his hands shook as he glared at the soldier, a man his very own age. He snarled at the thought that he'd had a life of plenty while Kael and his sister were sentenced to a life of starvation and slavery. The caste system, that's how. Kael and Zyla both had been unfortunate enough to be born into this social status. The lowest on the proverbial rung, with no way to grasp the upper rungs.

He'd been so careful and had almost made it back to the one room shack that he and Zyla called home. Damn it! He knew it was risky venturing into the woods. It was against the laws that the Elite set but he was so sick of being hungry and watching Zyla get weaker and weaker every day. There had to be something to eat in the woods, but the guard screwed that up. He hated the patrols and the constant feeling of being watched

The soldier unzipped his pants and sighed as the steam rose up from the growing puddle in front of him. Kael watched his every move as he casually stood unaware. If there was any time to make his move it would be now. His fist squeezed tighter; his knuckles white from the grip he had on the handle of the small homemade hatchet.

It wasn't a typical weapon, Grays weren't allowed weapons, but many made their own. The hatchet blade he'd crafted from stone and sharpened enough to split wood. The handle was from a thick stick of maple. It took him months of tedious work to knap the blade, but the end result was a weapon that was sharp and deadly.

The muscles in his legs quivered ready to launch him at the man but he held himself back, fighting the urge to attack the man. He didn't want to have to kill the soldier. He would if he had to. A soft growl tickled the back of his throat.

If it weren't for Zyla, he could easily leap upon him and with a murderous rage exact vengeance for all of the injustices.

With a breath trapped deep in his lungs, Kael watched the guard from his hiding spot, daring not to even breathe fearing the guard would hear him. It wasn't long before the guard stomped out his cigarette and walked back toward the village. Kael let out a shaky breath and waited a few minutes to be sure the guard was well out of sight before he climbed to his feet. Glancing nervously around he gathered his hatchet and brushed off the mud from his knees and made his way back toward Rysa.

Chapter Two

Kael's mind spun deep into the rabbit hole of despair, thoughts of Zyla once again waking up with no food, another day hungry. Desperation seized him; he just had to find her something other than the scrawny squirrel.

Consumed with feelings of self-doubt he walked slowly back to the shack hanging his head, his shoulders bowed, he was lost in his own thoughts. He followed the well-worn path between the shanty homes, grooved deep into the slush and mud, circling around the square and back to the shack.

Early spring blanketed the area, slender blades of grass poked sparsely through the thawing ground. Memories of his mother tugged at him. She was always excited for this time of year. What made it so special he scowled?

He stopped and looked up with wide eyes. He remembered why she was so happy for springtime. Dandelions... Although too early for them to push up through the ground, he remembered a patch that grew every year along the side of the small shack. They weren't given seeds to plant but some of the wild growth was edible. Perhaps, he wondered, maybe the ground has thawed enough for him to dig the roots? He was just desperate enough to try.

Her teachings wandered through his

thoughts as he walked. She'd tried to show him what they could eat, he looked around the village with new eyes. All the shacks looked alike. No paint, just rough boards loosely nailed to a rickety frame, identically fashioned into small one room sheds. They weren't even fit for animals, never mind humans. Each, haphazardly put together, barely standing, some leaning into others. Poverty was evident in every shambled yard and curtain-less window. Sooty smoke poured into the morning sky from tin pipes sticking out of the roofs of those that had scavenged materials for actual stoves. Others simply had a hole in the roof for the smoke of open fires on the dirt floor. He took in this scene of their meager existence and for the first time he fully understood and really felt the sting of all this injustice; it left him feeling desolate and hopeless.

His pace slowed when he approached his own small structure. His parents were smart; they had shoved mud into the cracks between the boards. His father called it chinking. He missed them both desperately on days like this. The days before the supplies would come were the worst. He knew the dandelions grew along the sunny side wall and he knelt beside it and clawed into the dirt, his cold fingers crying out in searing pain. Anger welled up inside him as he dug for the roots he knew to be there, hidden deep in the soil. His breath clouded the air with white puffs as he struggled, feeling the dirt compact painfully under his fingernails. The knees of his pants were soaked and cold, the slushy mud seeping through the thin, worn material.

A light shuffle halted the furious digging. The sound drew his attention from the ground to a woman passing on the other side of a small rickety fence. He dared not gaze in her direction, but a reflection of light danced on the muddy hole he'd been digging in. When he instinctively looked up to find its source, his eyes caught the shimmer of sparkle. A dragonfly dangled on a small string necklace, dancing in the sunlight. He said nothing, mesmerized by the sparkling and watched as she passed. She saw him and grimaced at his filthy appearance, wrinkling her nose when her eyes connected with his. She nodded to the ground and he quickly turned away. She shuffled hastily, crossing the muddy street.

He looked at the spot where she stood. Something sat at the edge of his small shack. In the place she'd nodded sat a small package, wrapped in brown paper. Curious, he reached out and picked it up. A glance in either direction was prudent before he unwrapped it; just a little to sneak a peek at the contents. He sucked in a quick breath when he saw that it was two pieces of meat. He looked across the street in the direction she'd gone, confusion etched on his face to find the woman was nowhere in sight.

He tucked the package beneath his worn jacket, stood and gazed around the neighborhood. Anxiety clawed at his stomach, he wondered and worried if anyone had seen him pick up the package. Questions emerged in his mind, should he try to find the woman and return it? She'd obviously dropped in on accident. She might recall him digging and accuse him of taking it. His noisy stomach argued the logic, Zyla was starving. He could make a stew with this and the roots he'd dug.

Indecision tore at him. If the woman noticed her package missing and accused him, then he could be charged with theft even though she'd dropped it. Just picking it up would implicate him. She was clearly a Brown; the Honor Guard would believe her before him if she accused him of stealing her package. Agonizing over the different thoughts made him paranoid. His eyes jerked from right to left looking for any observers who would have seen him and his teeth worried his bottom lip as indecision paralyzed his actions. He stared for a moment down at his dirty hands, the crust of imbedded mud under his fingernails.

No more indecision he chided himself, Zyla needed food. He'd face the consequences if he had to. With renewed resolve he reached for the long white roots of the dandelions, snatched them up and hurried through the entry to the small structure and his hungry sister. He glanced over his shoulder one last time before slipping inside and closing the door behind him

Calix

Calix watched from the shadowed corner of the old brick building that was once a church. A thick choking haze from the wood burning stoves drifted across the silent village. He shivered in his light jacket as he watched Kael move toward his front door, glance over his shoulder, then let himself in.

A cruel, hate-filled glint shone in his eyes. His fists clenched by his sides. Kael reminded him of the rats that came out at night, scampering their fat, little bodies across the floor, scavenging every crumb of food that inadvertently slipped from a shaking hand and onto the filthy floor. Loathing burned deep in his heart, palpable, seething, and blinding. And Zyla, Kael's spoilt rotten, precious little sister. He despised her even more. His tongue flicked out against his parched lips as he thought of the girl; her mousy brown hair, those big eyes that melted everyone around her. Everyone, but not him. He didn't fall for it. She wasn't the innocent her brother and others thought her to be. In fact, she was a conniving, little tease. Years back when they all played together, she'd teased him once too often pretending to like his short curly hair and then laughing because it looked like springs when she'd stretch it out and let it go. But he'd fix her; she'd pay for getting him into trouble and costing him three points. It was her fault that he'd been pushed down to a six. He was almost a brown before she told the guard he'd lied to them about the fire. He'd set the fire at the edge of the woods a year back to keep her warm while they chatted one chilly afternoon. Her stupid innocence. She just blurted it out when they grabbed her and cost him for the fire and the lie

"I'll show you what happens to snitches, you little mouse," he muttered.

Although he would never be able to touch her, he knew who would. Captain Akakin! And he would enjoy making her scream, just like her whore of a mother. The thought pleased Calix. He stood in silent contemplation as he wiped away a thin line of drool from his bottom lip with the back of his hand. It was time… Time for him to set his plan into motion and collect the reward promised. He was sick of being hungry all the time and the promise of more food and more fuel for his fire, not only offered more comforts but revenge. If he did just this one thing; the thoughts of reward made the effort of pretending around Kael and Zyla more bearable. A small grin emerged; he knew how to get them. Anxious to gain his favor, he turned on his heels briskly walking against the early morning chill. On a mission, he made his way toward the Honor Guard garrison.

One quick rap of his knuckles against the wooden door and it opened with a creak of rusty hinges. He looked up into the cold eyes of First Rank Guard, Keifer.

"What in the hell do you want boy?" Keifer growled.

A gust of wind crawled down the collar of his jacket, brushing the skin beneath his shirt as he stood in the doorway, making him shiver. The guard's breath smelled like rotted meat. It wafted to Calix's nose causing him to gag. He struggled to keep from showing the disgust that roiled up in his gut as he spoke. "I need to see Captain Akakin, please," Calix replied.

He watched Keifer's face, the spite rising up as it darkened with malice. "You need? How does it feel to need lowlife?" Keifer snarled.

Calix winced when Keifer's hand snaked out and cuffed him hard on his ear. "I'm sorry First Rank to bother you on this fine morning sir," Calix moaned as he lowered his head. "But Captain Akakin is expecting me sir," Calix replied, ignoring the ringing in his ear from the blow.

Barely daring to glance upward he saw Keifer's eyes narrow suspiciously. "I'll check with him. If you're lying, I'm gonna make you regret it boy," he snarled jabbing him in the chest with the handle of a whip he carried around.

Calix nodded, his hands clasped together, eyes cast downward. In his heart he seethed with anger. One day he would kill him, he promised himself.

Kael

Kael sniffed tiredly; a chill he couldn't seem to shake penetrated his body bone deep. He blew a warm breath into his cold hands and glanced at Zyla. She was awake and staring up at him from beneath her covers.

"It's cold in here brother," she whimpered.

He nodded slowly; they were out of wood completely. All that they had left was the straw and branches they used for bedding.

"Get up, I'll feed the stove with our bedding and get some heat in here," he replied.

She smiled slightly as she pulled the thin blankets tighter around her and pushed herself up from the floor. Her long brown hair was tousled around her head and he watched as she gathered it up into a bun and pinned it with a straight stick. Her hollowed eyes dark with fatigue and hunger only lent an air of beauty to her face, much like their mother. God, he missed her; missed his dad too. A tug jolted his heart as he looked at Zyla. He had to protect her. Somehow, some way he had to protect her from what he knew was to come. The thought of the Honor Guard coming for her shattered his heart. The very thought of it felt like sharp shards of glass ripping at his chest angering him as he snapped the small branches into a manageable size.

"I'm hungry, maybe Mischa will have something to spare?" she said, half question, half hope.

Mischa, their neighbor, and Zyla's best friend, lived by herself. Both of her parents had died earlier that year, leaving the sixteen-year-old girl to fend for herself. She'd fared well though, squirreling away food and supplies, keeping it hidden from the Honor Guard. She often shared her food with Zyla and others she trusted.

"No, don't bother Mischa," Kael snapped.

He saw his sister glance at him imploringly while he continued to get the fire going. "But Kael, I'm so hungry," she moaned.

She understood his hesitancy in begging others, especially Mischa, for food. It hurt his manhood. He was supposed to be taking care of them both and he looked upon begging as a reflection of his own failure.

"I have something for you," he said as he pulled the package from beneath his coat and the squirrel he'd caught in his traps. He watched as Zyla's eyes lit up when she saw the two pieces of meat.

"Where did you get those?" she squealed

"Better for you not to know," he said.

Turning, he scooped up a few handfuls of straw, a couple more pine boughs from her bedding and fed them into the wood stove. He could feel the beginnings of real heat as the stove warmed up. Kael shook his head as if it were no big thing and tossed the small pot on the stove and began to cut up the roots and meat into a bit of water. Zyla looked into the pot with anticipation as it began to boil on the now growing fire.

"You didn't steal from someone did you?" Zyla asked, her mouth watering.

Kael shook his head, grinning at her. His mouth watered as the smell of cooking meat rose up from the pot. Cut into small pieces it cooked swiftly. He reached in with the spoon and retrieved a chunk of the meat, passing it to her. She ate it hungrily, sucking air over her teeth to cool the steaming hot morsel. He watched her greedily eating it, smiling slightly as she tried to chew the piping hot food.

"You need to eat too brother," she said softly holding out the spoon to him.

He didn't want to take it. He wanted her to have it all, but his stomach rumbled from the hunger that gnawed at him. He took the spoon, shoving it into his mouth and he too sucked the air over his teeth to cool the savory bites. They both laughed at one another's awkward chewing, but the food felt like the best meal they'd ever had. Each felt refreshed and strengthened

He turned his back for Zyla to dress. She shivered; her frail body exposed to the draft as she pulled off her nightclothes. Her ribs protruded under her pasty white skin making her look ghost-like. She grabbed her clothes and moved closer, standing near the heat of the wood stove to dress. She pulled a gray, tattered smock over her head then threw on a sweater to cover her arms. When she was done, she made her way to the basin of frigid water and splashed her face.

"I am doing laundry today for one of the Honor Guard," she said as she dried her face with the hem of her dress. "I'll probably get enough for another meal." She said excitedly.

Kael scowled. He hated that she had to take on jobs such as doing laundry for the members of the Honor Guard in order to earn a scrap of food. They're only doing it to check her out because she would be fifteen soon. They were using her for the time that she is underage like she was some common slave or personal maid to those pigs.

"I hate that you go there," he hissed angrily. His gaze softened, "I just don't want them to see you so much. You know what happened to Mischa. I don't want that to happen to you."

He saw her nod then shrug her shoulders. "I know. But what else is there to do? We're out of food, we're out of wood, our allotment won't be in for another two days," she replied. "At least with the duties today, perhaps the First Rank, Bevin, will give me enough to hold us over," she explained.

First Rank Bevin wasn't as bad as some of the other Honor Guard soldiers. He at least didn't try to paw at her or cajole her into other more intimate favors in trade for food. She could stand him more than some of the others she'd performed work for.

"He's a pig, just like the others," Kael snapped.

Although he hated the fact that she had to work for the Honor Guard, he understood why she did it. Without her picking up work here and there, they surely would have starved long ago. He too had work ahead of him today. A family in the green sector on the east side of town needed more wood cut. They didn't have to do it themselves, with their status as greens, but the brown status workers thought wood cutting was beneath them, that it was gray work. They could afford to hire it out, because they were almost to yellow and that is some real high status. None of them had been below a green. Birth score seemed unfair. He was born at an eight because that was his family score. He knew they would pay him a pittance, but it was better than nothing. They promised him five sticks of firewood if he stacked them a cord. Five lousy sticks. But he'd accepted the work none the less. Five sticks were better than freezing to death.

They each had their communal work to do as well and he didn't want her wearing herself down with the extra tasks.

"Okay, so you'll be done in a few hours?" he asked, a heavy trace of worry in his voice.

She nodded and gave him a reassuring weak smile as her hands nervously worked to smooth the wrinkles from her smock. "I promise, I'll be back in a few hours," she replied.

He watched as she walked out the front door, her shoulders slumped under the pressure of the heavy duties before her. He clenched his jaw in frustration and his fists curled at his side.

Zyla

Thankful that Kael had made stew that morning and the extra energy it gave her. She walked along sniffing the morning air. Spring was coming and the winter would finally end. A sound rustling in the bushes frightened her, she paused and felt like someone was watching her. A loud snap from behind startled her and she ran to the garrison. She was always terrified that someone would snatch her after seeing what Akakin had done to the young girl on her birthday. She knew hers was only a month away and what it meant. It made her jumpy and filled her with anxiety. Each day she awoke and counted the days, dreading the day it would be hers. Panicked she ran to the garrison feeling as though someone were watching her sent a chill down her spine.

She wasn't going to let it spoil her day, she liked Bevin; he always gave her the best scraps from the kitchen. Her sack would be full today with food, wood, and even some soap if she were lucky. Springtime had a way of brightening even a gray morning. She arrived and got to work on his washing right away. The thought of the rustling bush gave her mind something to work on while her hands were occupied.

The rustle in the bushes reminded her of the day she found her very own pet. Of course, Kael would disapprove but she kept it anyway. That day just over a month ago the same bushes rustled with life. A weak peep caught her ear and she knew it was no person. Slowly she'd parted the branches to find a frightened pair of eyes staring at her. It was a hawk. He was beautiful. Her eyes sparkled and she reached out for it. It let out a feeble squawk and tried to back away from her only tangling itself further in the bush. She cooed at it and gently touched the soft feathers, finally bringing it out of the tangle and into the sunlight. The hawk struggled to get away, but his wing was injured. She cooed at it again and gently placed it in her basket. She'd been standing in front of the wash bin, wringing clothes with a small smile, not aware that Bevin had come in.

"How's the laundry going?"

It startled her from her thoughts of the hawk, and she stuttered, "ummmm."

He was kind and his eyes smiled in appreciation for all the wash hanging on the lines and said she could go.

The day went swiftly and as she'd hoped Bevin filled her sack with four sticks of wood, three bundles of wrapped up scraps, a piece of meat that was nearly the size of her fist and a few smaller pieces, along with a small jar of real milk. She thanked him and hurried out the door for home. She was excited to show Kael but possibly more so to share some food with her pet.

Behind the small shack was a juniper bush. Where she pulled the contents out of her sack. The basket that she'd said she'd lost was placed inside the bush almost completely upside down. The small rag she used to cover her basket was now filthy, laid out on the ground inside the covering. She gently reached out to the bird inside the shelter with a small piece of biscuit. It looked to where she'd set the tiny morsel of meat. She knew what it wanted and reached for the meat. She pulled it from the wrapping and held it out to the bird who snapped at it. She stared at the meat, a meager portion, and knew it would make a stew for them, there were still days to go before food would arrive. "If Kael finds you, he'll want to put you into a stew," she whispered to her feathered friend.

She felt bad that Kael would worry for food, but she had more and even still offered the bird the chunk of meat which it ate hungrily.

She smiled at it and hushed it, "You stay quiet and I'll be back later." Then lowered the basket back over it and went inside. She'd simply cut the larger piece into two portions and he could make stew out of that.

She was not wrong when she felt as though someone were watching her. Creed's keen eye followed her every movement. Each day he would watch her go to and from the garrison, his watchful eye vigilant to danger. But this day he was observing more than her tender moment with the animal. Behind the next shack stood another onlooker, the lighter color of his curls shone like a beacon to him. He noted how the onlooker had a look of savagery and lust.

When the figure retreated into the alley between the houses Creed relaxed his bow and his gaze fell back to Zyla. A small smile emerged watching her tender hand with the animal. Realizing he'd been smiling, he scoffed, "Stupid girl, the bird would make a fine meal." He turned and retreated into the woods.

Chapter Three

Kael stood in front of the woodstove, desperately trying to capture any heat from the barely burning embers to warm his hands. He stood motionless except for the shaking from the cold. His eyes flashed a deadly nervous glance at the front door. Zyla's birthday was just over a week away and it had him edgy and angry. He could barely control the rising rage each time the thoughts of exactly what that meant crept in and inserted itself into his thoughts.

The frigid air that slithered between the boards into the tiny shack, chilled his skin when he took off his worn, ragged shirt. He wanted to feel the sting of its icy touch. Zyla was working again for Bevin. Her absence gave him time to practice with the rough-cut staff he'd fashioned from a long sapling. On either end, it was sharpened to a fine and deadly point. Testing its weight and balance in his hands, turning it over and hefting it, he was pleased with its feel. Without any warning he made a lunge at an unseen enemy, the same way he'd done a thousand times before. He was getting faster, more agile, spinning the staff in his hands, using the weapon as though it were an extension of his own arms and hands.

He danced the dance of death; the one he knew would someday come. Thrusting, twirling, spinning on his feet gracefully, dodging imagined blows. His chest, arms and shoulders glistened with sweat. His breath panted in and out lightly and rapidly. His thoughts transporting him into a time when he knew this dance would be a reality. The day that he would stand in the entrance of the arena as his father had done those many years ago. He didn't want to think about it, he'd been planning and seeking a way to save them both.

The training helped take his mind off of other things, but today anger pulsed in his ears, a heartbeat all its own as he thought of how Captain Akakin had been sniffing around Zyla like a dog in heat, how his eyes followed her hungrily. The way he'd made her feel just trying to get through each day's work.

He froze, the knock on the door startled him; he wasn't expecting anyone. Sucking in a deep breath, he quickly shoved the staff under his sleeping mat and then threw his shirt on. He paused with his hand on the latch, struggling to calm his breath. His mind ran through a dozen scenarios as he opened the door a fraction and peeked out. Calix stood on the front porch, hands deep in his pockets, turned facing outward, his gaze staring across the street.

"Come in friend," Kael said, opening the door wider.

His foot held the door from opening

too wide, as Calix walked through. Before closing it, he cast a nervous glance toward the street; curious to see what he was looking at.

The morning air was frosty, but thankfully not the bitter cold of the winter. The tender warmth of spring was right on the doorstep. He could smell it, taking in a deep breath the earthy aroma of renewed life energized him. Calix stood at the stove rubbing his hands together to warm them over the meager heat of the stove.

"I saw Akakin again, he was scoping out your house," Calix muttered as he glanced around the room.

It made Kael nervous having even Calix in their shack. His staff, that was forbidden, and the few supplies they'd gotten for extra work could make them a target.

"Where is she?" Calix asked, worriedly.

Kael shook his head. "She's working again today at the garrison. Bevin keeps her busy," Kael replied.

"And you? Are you watching her?" Calix snapped.

Kael growled low in his throat, wiping a sheen of sweat from his face. "Of course I'm watching her! But what can I do? She's got to take on the work; she's got to perform her services just like everyone else!" Kael snapped.

His friend's question irritated him. Mostly because it rubbed in the fact that he was utterly helpless to change the situation.

"And Mischa? What is up with that girl? I heard Keifer has been asking about her," Calix spat.

Kael saw the grimace cross his friend's face. Keifer was a little more than interested in Mischa lately. Kael couldn't help but wonder why; Mischa had already been going to Akakin's quarters. He turned, his face hiding just how pissed off he was about Keifer's interest in Mischa. All of the girls in his area were abused by the guard; it made his blood sizzle with hatred. Keifer was known to be extra rough on the girls.

"I don't know where she is; it's not my responsibility to watch her." Kael venomously snapped back.

His gaze avoided looking at his friend. He did know but he'd be damned if he'd tell anyone Mischa's whereabouts. She had a habit of evading trouble… and she was damn good at it. He wasn't going to help Calix or Keifer one iota.

A chill raised goose bumps on Kael's arms, and he pulled his jacket around his shoulders. He could feel Calix's eyes on him, but he ignored him.

"Well, if you see her, warn her. Tell her that Keifer is in a dangerous mood, and she'd better be on guard. If he gets to her with the mood he's in, she's gonna be in for a beating," Calix warned.

Kael nodded. He would tell her. The thought of what Keifer was capable of doing curled his stomach. After Calix left, Kael slipped out the back side. They had a loose board their father kept secure with a small wire for escaping. Kael had taken to using it regularly on his explorations. He needed to talk with Mischa. If their plan was to work, he needed to warn her about Keifer. He didn't need him getting his hands on her. It would ruin everything.

He crept silently through the woods. It still felt terrifying although for the past few weeks he'd been going to the darkly shadowed forest. The weather was turning warmer, but spring had one consequence, the ground was thawing, and mud seeped through the holes in his boots and turned his toes to ice. At the perching rock, he whistled sharply twice and waited. The morning sun filtered through the skeletal branches of the tree. Their shadows danced in eerie unison on the ground.

He glanced around nervously, his senses on full alert, he could never be sure that no one had seen him. The soft snapping sound of a stick made the hairs stand up on the back of his neck. It alerted him to a presence, Mischa's presence.

He watched her graceful movements as she stepped out from behind a large oak tree. His eyes rested on her easily and a sigh of relief and appreciation escaped his lips. Her long golden hair hung in a single braid down her back, secured with a strip of rag. She wore pants, forbidden for women, which showed the curves of her slender frame. On her side she carried a dagger, sheathed in leather and attached to her belt with a cord of twine. She moved as silently as a soft breeze, almost gliding as she walked toward him. A smile lit her face, making his heart skip when he looked into her pale blue eyes.

"Keifer's looking for you," Kael said blandly, trying to masque his thoughts of her. It was hard to hide as his eyes took in her flushed face. She glanced at him, smiled, and nodded.

"I'm almost ready," she said excitedly. "Another day and we can get Zyla away from this place," her voice softened.

Kael sighed deeply. What Mischa was doing was dangerous for them all. If she were caught, then it would surely mean her imprisonment and possible death. Death would be the easiest. As a prisoner, it took all rights and status away from her and would mean she would be accessible to every man in the village along with every soldier at the garrison. She would be reduced to nothing but an animal, a non-entity. She would suffer greatly, and this troubled Kael.

"Be careful Mischa, just please be careful," he said as he pulled her into his arms and kissed the top of her head. He loved her. Plain and simple. Although it wasn't allowed, they took great care to hide it, it was there none the less. He felt her body press into his and he smelled the fresh air and sunshine in her hair.

"You worry too much Kael," she said as she nuzzled her face against his neck, "I've got help. There are people on our side," she reassured him.

He grimaced, not quite believing the stories she'd told him. If there were people helping them, then where the hell are they? With a deep sigh, not wanting to let her go, he released his arms from her and felt the absence of warmth as she stepped away from him.

"You just keep that pig Akakin away from her while I finish up my business," she hissed, her eyes narrowing with anger.

Akakin was the worst, worse than Keifer even. She'd dealt with Keifer before and handled him. But there would be no handling Akakin. That man was mean; he took pleasure in the suffering of others. A shiver coursed through her just thinking about what he would do to Zyla; her sweet nature, he would soil it with his sadistic actions. She couldn't let that happen, not to Zyla.

Kael nodded. "I promise that pig will never get his hands on my sister!" he growled.

He watched relief spread across Mischa's face. He didn't know, didn't want to know what she'd been through at the hands of Keifer and Akakin. There was a lot he didn't want to know. And he would never ask her. In the village, talking of what went on behind the closed doors of the garrison was taboo. It was enough that every woman in the village carried the shame of their status, never mind the shame of what the guardsmen forced them to do as personal servants and slaves to their every whim. No, he would never dishonor her by asking and she would never dishonor herself by telling. It was best left unsaid.

Zyla

Kael emerged from the woods finding Zyla crouched behind the shack. He walked right up on her without her hearing him. That made him angry and he shouted at her, "Zyla!"

She jumped up and spun around facing him, terror in her eyes. "Oh, Kael, you scared me." She shuffled her feet and moved to the left to hide the basket.

"What were you doing?" he scolded. "Someone could have attacked you."

"I'm sorry," she sighed. "I must have been distracted."

"What were you doing down there anyway?" he asked, shoving his way past her.

"Kael wait," she protested.

Kael lifted the basket to find the Hawk nestled inside. It gazed up at him confused. This wasn't the face it was used to seeing. He stepped back and looked at her, first confused then angry. "How long?"

"Uh, well…" she muttered

"How long has this thing been eating our food Zyla?" he demanded.

"I found it a few weeks ago," she lied. "And it was hurt so I brought it home and took care of it," she stammered.

Kael's eyes lit up, "do you know how many meals…"

Zyla cut him off before he could finish. "No Kael, you can't… I won't," she protested. "I won't feed it anymore; I was just getting ready to see if it could fly again anyway." She pleaded with him.

Kael hated it when she did that; his heart would go soft gazing into her big teary-eyed cry for him to do this or that. She knew it made him give in and used it every time. He slammed the basket down on the ground. "Get rid of it," he growled. "If it is here tonight, it's dinner. You got me?"

"I will," she promised.

Kael threw the basket aside and stomped off into the shack. "I mean it Zyla." She heard him call out from inside.

Zyla bent down to the bird and cooed, it cooed back at her as she stroked it's back. "You'll have to go now."

She stood up and walked toward the tree line cradling her short-lived pet, her little feathered friend. She opened her arms to let the bird go but it didn't fly. She knew the wing had healed; she'd seen the bird stretch out its wings for her.

She encouraged it, "go, shoo."

Still it sat in her arms refusing to leave her. She hoisted her hands up and down to get the bird to fly. Wings spread, it simply hopped about in her hands. Finally, she tossed the bird into the air and it flew. She knew it could. She smiled at the hawk soaring overhead and waved it goodbye. When she waved, it returned and perched on the branch above her. She smiled and watched it dance on the limb for a few moments.

Creed leaned in to see where the bird had gone and snapped a small branch. He jerked himself back behind the large rock and sat silent. After a few moments he peered around the rock and saw that she was retrieving her basket and cloth from the shrub. "I ought to shoot that bird out of the sky and teach her a lesson," he mumbled to himself. Then he looked back to her and watched her small figure stand tip toed trying to regain sight of the animal.

His heart thumped in his chest staring at her slender figure leaning into the sun to see her friend. His breath caught in his chest when she tripped over the small shrub rounding the corner of the shack. The urge to catch her nearly overpowered his need to stay hidden. "Stupid girl," he muttered and turned, disappearing into the woods.

Calix

He stood in front of Captain Akakin nervously wringing his hands. His head bowed, staring at his feet, contemplating how fast they could run away, while only half listening to the tirade of angry words and insults hurled at him. His heart started to beat rapidly in fear as he sensed the Captain's anger. He'd been sent to find out the whereabouts of Mischa and to check on Zyla. Well, at least he could tell the Captain about Zyla, the little tease. That might dampen the captain's anger a bit. Lifting his face, he looked directly at Akakin, his gaze unwavering even though the fear welling up in the pit of his belly was nearly overwhelming.

"He's telling me nothing, sir," he

muttered in his own defense. "Zyla is here today. Right here at the garrison, working for Bevin. I do fear he may be winning favor with her and will bed her before you do," he hissed, sensing his position with Akakin strengthening. He continued, laying it on thicker. "With your authority Sir, you shouldn't have any problem calling her away from him. Right?" Calix suggested. Calix needed this to work. He needed that fat pig Akakin to make his move on Zyla. It was the only way to set Baylin's plan into motion.

He thought of the woman, Baylin, and smiled tightly. She hated Kael and his sister almost as much as he did. He didn't know why she hated them, and it didn't matter to him. She was paying him and paying him well for his part in this plan. He'd never seen the woman, but he was sure this could be a Godsend. His only contact with her was through one of her servants, Nova. He was a young boy of about sixteen; skinny and gangly, almost effeminate. He didn't like the boy, but that didn't matter and he kept it to himself. He certainly didn't want to upset Baylin.

As an Elite, Baylin had the status needed to send Kael to the Arena. She only needed a reason. That was up to Calix to provide. Whether it be catching him stealing, or the off chance that he caught him wandering into the preserve. Whatever dirt he could dig up, true or not, if she could use it against Kael, it was useful information. This was an assignment Calix happily accepted. A grunt from Captain Akakin brought him back to the moment, jerking him from his thoughts of reward and luxury.

"Get out of my office," he exclaimed. "Now boy, before I skin you alive," Akakin barked flailing his hands in the air, shooing him like a bird that had stayed at the feeder too long.

Calix nodded over and over, as he backed out the door. But now, he would watch. The idea had been planted and he saw Akakin's eyes flicker with interest. The man tried hard not to show it, but he knew it was there. After closing the door, Calix smiled. Now he would just wait and see.

Akakin

After he sent the boy off, Akakin sat behind his desk and pondered the situation. He absently picked at a scab on his face as his imagination filled his mind with ideas. If only he could somehow get the girl alone. It needed to be away from that brother of hers and then he'd be able to take her early. He'd been watching Zyla for the past few weeks, he knew she was nearly fifteen and was just biding his time. What Calix had said was stuck in his mind. What if the boy was right and Bevin had set his sights on her? He'd have to make his move before her birthday.

The general would bust him down to errand boy or worse, send him to the arena if he broke the age rule. They could get away with the abuse but there was a line they couldn't cross. Things like murder and rape were serious and the only way around it so far was to give them things in return. The rules on age were absolute, no one under fifteen or over sixty. There was no longer anyone over sixty the Grays never lived that long. If someone told, he'd be done for.

The racing of thoughts in his mind angered him. He slammed his fist on the desk, there was no way he was going to let one of the guardsmen get to her before he got his chance. He was first and they all knew it, he'd make sure they remembered that. Thinking of her and how he'd been waiting these past few months since the coming birthdays came across his desk. Yes, the new girls were always the most fun to play with he nodded to himself. He became agitated thinking about how he would handle Bevin.

His men knew the rules, but many tried to skirt them and often got away with it, but not this one… This one he had plans for. He looked at the palm of his hand where a long scar ran through. "Her mother… She did this to me, and now her daughter will pay."

His eyes shrunk to slits as he sneered.

Thus far he'd closed his eyes to most of the shenanigans that went on between his men and the village women. He knew there was plenty of rule bending. But when it came to his possessions, and he considered the unbroken girls his possession until he decided who to keep. Here he drew the line. The thought of Bevin taking first shot at Zyla angered him. How dare that lowly First Rank think he could get away with it? The silver bell sat on his desk, daring him to do something about it. He snatched it with malice and rang it loudly.

His assistant came shuffling in. "Yes Sir?" the older man asked.

Akakin glanced at him, taking in the wrinkled, dirty uniform. He didn't say anything, just raised an eyebrow and looked him up and down. The man knew he noticed and nervously shifted from one foot to another. "Go get First Rank Bevin. I want to see him," he ordered.

He watched as the unkempt man bowed his head and backed out the door. The proper sign of respect from a lower status foot soldier.

A few minutes later, First Rank Bevin entered his office and cleared his throat to announce himself. Akakin knew he was there already. He placed the pen carefully on the desk and leaned back in his chair and glared at him. The man looked uncomfortable, even nervous and that was exactly the way Akakin wanted him to feel.

"I'll get right to the point Bevin," Akakin said as he stood and walked around his desk.

He was a good six inches shorter than Bevin and much rounder, but he carried himself with an air of complete confidence and authority. He coughed lightly into his hand and drew his shoulders up straight, trying to appear taller than he actually was.

"Please, take a seat." He motioned toward the chair in front of the desk. This would remove the uncomfortable tallness of the man.

For some reason, Bevin irritated him… always had. It was probably the man's cool demeanor, his air of superiority. He scoffed at the very thought of it. He hadn't picked Bevin for his unit. He was sent to him by Asha. Here was a woman he had little respect for, but because she was in the top tier of those with elite scores, he knew it best to appease her. She was about as high up as a person could get and angering her was never good for status.

"I see that you are using the village girl for laundry and cleaning services, ummm what's her name?"

"Yes Sir, Zyla Sir." Bevin said.

"Oh yeah, Zyla," Akakin said.

Bevin nodded and looked at him coolly. "Yes sir, I find that she does a better job than most." He sat waiting for a reason for this, wondering just where in the hell Akakin was going with it. Red flags of suspicion screamed in his mind and his gut clenched nervously. He despised this man and had a very hard time keeping that emotion off of his face. He swallowed an uneasy, greasy feeling in his gut.

"Well, I want you to stop using her," Akakin said matter of factly. "She's too undernourished, too weak, and I'm worried about her," Akakin lied.

He grasped Bevin shoulder firmly, as a friend would, tight enough to let Bevin know his strength and smiled. "She's such a little thing ya know?" he said.

Bevin nodded, holding back the bile that kissed the back of his throat. The old goat didn't care one whit for anyone but himself, much less some random Gray. No, there was something much slicker and slimier going on, something behind his request and Bevin had a sneaking suspicion that he knew what it was.

He knew Zyla's birthday was soon. He also knew that Akakin prided himself on first taste of each new girl when they came of age. This thought made his skin crawl and his hands itch to reach out and strangle the life out of just one more worthless piece of trash.

He knew he had to keep his cool. "But sir," he said softly. "If you don't mind me being so bold?" He hesitated a moment and looked at Akakin trying to appear concerned. "I feel that by having her do some work, she'll get the chance at more food." Raised eyebrows offered the illusion of concern for his appearance.

"Mmhmm" Akakin nodded without real interest.

"I pay her in scraps you know, and I don't work her too hard; just enough to remind her who's boss and where her place is in this hierarchy," Bevin finished, hoping his cool attitude kept the captain from suspecting his real reasons for requesting Zyla exclusively.

He requested her exclusively because he knew the other men would find a way to get to her. This was how he kept her safe. If she were under his watch, they wouldn't dare. He was well known among his brethren for his vicious temper. A temper he didn't hesitate to use should anyone piss him off or cross him.

"I understand this, but even what light duties you are giving her are too much. No, I insist she not work for you anymore," Akakin said, his eyes narrowing to push his point home.

Bevin nodded in a bow. "Very well sir, I'll release her from my requests for the rest of the week."

His heart lurched with fear for the young girl. He succeeded in protecting her from others in the garrison, but he'd not be able to save her from Akakin. This thought tore into his heart. He hated this caste system, hated it with every cell in his body.

"Very good, you're dismissed. I've got some other business I need to attend to," Akakin said. He dismissed Bevin with a wave of his fat, pudgy hand. He felt satisfied that the First Rank would do exactly as he was told.

Before Bevin closed the door, Akakin shouted to him once more. "Oh, I forgot to ask you. What time are you releasing her today?"

Bevin glanced darkly at the captain. "In one hour sir," he replied.

"Ok," Akakin said, unceremoniously waving his hand at him to leave.

Bevin shut the door. He had an uneasy, foreboding feeling about Akakin.

Calix

Calix stood, leaning against the wrought iron fence in front of the garrison. His work for the day finished, not that it was that hard to begin with. He had it in good with the guardsmen, thanks to Baylin. She'd instructed them to provide him with extra rations for very little work and they didn't dare challenge her. He saw Captain Akakin lounging in a rocking chair, on the front deck of the old historic manor, his legs splayed out in front of him like a great whale. The sun finally warmed up the afternoon and it actually felt springtime comfortable. Calix raised his face to the warmth of the sun breathing in the fresh air. He cast a glance every so often toward the Captain, but not so much as to come under his scrutiny.

He could tell, and so could everyone else, that the Captain was up to something. He noticed that the man's eyes every so often would dart toward the door of Bevin's house. It was as if he were waiting for someone. Calix could take a good bet that he knew exactly who that someone was.

Sure enough, a few minutes later, he saw Zyla come strolling out the front door, a small bag in her hands. His eyes grew to hateful slits as he saw the smile on her face. That little tease had just finished her work for Bevin. Nonchalantly, he stepped away from the fence and strolled toward the side of the building where he could watch without being seen.

He leaned against the painted smooth wooden wall and bit his lower lip. Yes, it was just as he'd thought. He watched as Zyla bounced down the front steps and made her way onto the muddy street. Not far behind, followed Captain Akakin. Calix smiled coldly. His plan was working perfectly. He'd taken his suggestion earlier and decided to make his move on the girl. "Perfect," he hissed under his breath.

Calix turned on his heel. Almost excited, he skipped behind the garrison and took the small alley that snaked its way between the shacks towards Kael's house. Time to bring the boy into this little tete-a-tete, so he can see for himself. Grinning maliciously, he sped up his pace. He wouldn't want Kael to miss the first act now, not after all the hard work he did putting this little shindig together. He chuckled as he thought of how this stupid fool would respond to seeing that pig Akakin trailing his sister like a hungry hound.

He found Kael at a neighbor's house. He was on his hands and knees digging in the hard soil getting ready to plant for her. Calix wiped the smirk off his face and quickly practiced a worried look as he approached him.

He tugged at Kael's shoulder urgently. "You'd better come quick, Akakin is following your sister! I saw him leave the garrison right behind her," Calix growled, acting like he was worried and scared for Zyla.

Kael stood and threw the shovel onto the dirt, glaring at him. "Where did you see them?" he barked as he wiped his dirty hands down the front of his jeans and squinted into the afternoon sun. Rage rose up within him that he was unable to contain. He screamed at Calix, "where?"

Calix fought back a grin as he saw the anger darkening Kael's face. "Just outside of Beacon Way," Calix replied. His expression curious, not as though it were humorous but also not horrified by what was going on.

Kael's face was filled with rage, he knew this day would come and planned to get Zyla out of here, but it was too soon. He and Mischa had planned it all to take place before her birthday. He couldn't believe this was happening.

Kael turned and glared at Calix, "She's not even fifteen yet." He growled.

Calix followed as Kael took off running. "Don't do something stupid, Kael," Calix warned, although he knew something stupid was exactly what Kael would do.

Yes, his plan was unfolding perfectly. His heart slammed in his chest; he'd never had to run so fast in his life. He gasped and his breath heaved trying to get air into his lungs. The pace was incredible, but he had to keep up with Kael who was on a flat-out sprint. Damn that boy was fast when he needed to be.

Chapter Four

Zyla was happy with her earnings and excited to get home and show Kael. Her joy faded when she heard something behind her. She felt eyes on her as she walked but each time she turned to look, no one was there. She picked up her pace hurrying to get to what she thought was safety at home. Fear clutched at her throat when from the corner of her eye she spied Captain Akakin duck into a doorway when she turned. He was following her! Panic nearly overtook her. The man was fast for someone who was so grossly obese. Panic overwhelmed her and fear tightened in her chest as she tried to think clearly what to do. Her mind screamed danger. He wouldn't… would he? It wasn't her birthday yet. It was the law. He couldn't touch her. He was captain of the honor guard; he can't break the very laws he was sent to uphold. A sinking feeling in the pit of her stomach told her he would, and he'd think nothing of it.

She rounded the corner from Beacon Way onto a narrower mud track called Hellsman's Pass. A narrow alley with side by side little wooden shanties, packed in tight. It was a shortcut to home, but a mistake she'd instantly regret. She screamed when she felt a strong hand clamp down on her shoulder and spin her around.

"Hey little Zyla, what's your hurry?"

Captain Akakin purred as he pushed his face into hers.

Her eyes widened in fear and tears burst forth. She looked in either direction as her mind frantically scrambled for an escape.

"I'm not gonna hurt you." He cooed. "Well, not much," she heard him say then chuckle.

The sting of pain racked her body when he slammed her against the wooden wall of one of the shanties. Her breath exploded from her lungs with the force of the blow. She dropped the precious bag of food scraps she'd clung to desperately. She cried out in anguish when it broke open on the ground. Her first thought was pure anger at seeing the food scattered about and his clumsy large feet mashing it into the mud.

She found her voice and pleaded with him. "Please sir, Captain Akakin, please," she cried out helplessly.

He grinned and pinned her to the wall with his heavy body, he liked the terror he brought and fed on it. His putrid breath clogged her nostrils and gagged her.

"Please what my little butterfly?" he teased.

He bent his face toward her and was mere inches from her face. Zyla fought the dizziness in her mind and choked back a gag, wrenching her face away from his. He grabbed her face with his massive paw and jerked it back. Before she could scream he mashed his mouth onto hers in a punishing rough assault on her lips. She still tried to scream against his gut-wrenching kiss. With her free hand she reached up and scratched his cheek to get his face off of hers. He abruptly pulled away his hand reaching for the three bleeding scrapes down his cheek. Before she could get away, she saw his fist coming at her face and pain exploded behind her eyes when it impacted her cheekbone. She cried out throwing her arms up to shield her face.

"If you just hold still, this will be so much easier," Captain Akakin growled.

He struggled to subdue her while his hand tore at the front of her dress, dragging the hem upward. Silent sobs caught in her throat; she was screaming but nothing was coming out. He reached for her leggings and she squeezed her legs together, pummeling him with her small fists. The sun burned down upon her, blinding her in its brightness as her mind twisted its way inward, taking her from his ravaging assault. This couldn't be, she wasn't of age. But it was happening. The pain in her face, the roughness of his hands, the stench of his breath, all brought her back to the reality of the situation. She was trapped with no way out.

"I said, stop struggling bitch!" Captain Akakin growled into her ear as he pressed one of his legs between hers.

A screech pierced his ears just before her hawk swooped down and latched his talons into the man's back. Hopping up and down digging into him each time the bird tried valiantly to aid her.

She fought breathlessly; with every ounce of weak energy she could muster, she lashed out in defense. Another blow to her face rocked her head back and she tasted the salty, coppery tinge of blood in her mouth.

"Just like your mother!" she heard him growl as one of his hands grasped roughly onto her breast and squeezed hard. "She fought me too, but like her…there's nothing you can do." He laughed.

A moan bubbled up from the back of her throat, the pain driving her almost to her knees. Her nose bled and ran down her lips from his repeated punches to her face. She coughed back the urge to vomit as she choked on the blood trickling down her throat.

If he kept this up, she knew she would surely die. Darkness danced at the edge of her vision as his assault intensified. Her struggles weakened, her breath gasping in and out of her lungs with each blow. She no longer had the energy to cry out. She sobbed and sank to the ground. She was helpless to stop him; he was too powerful. Curling up, she let her mind drift away from the pain as he tore the back of her dress in two. Numbness descended on her.

Kael

Kael's breath rushed in and out as he ran, searching for Zyla. Panic gripping him, erasing all thoughts of hunger, fatigue, even sanity, he was blinded by rage. If that man touched her, laid on finger on her, he'd kill him and suffer the consequences. When he rounded the corner on Beacon he paused, frantically searching for her. A scream shattered the quiet street and he followed the sound down the alley toward Hellsman's Pass. His heart exploded in anguish when he recognized Zyla's fearful voice.

"Please Captain Akakin, please stop," he heard her cry. The shock of what he saw, the scene before him enraged him. A dark fury filled his mind when he saw Akakin ripping Zyla's dress from her body. That damn bird dancing and lashing out at the man's face. His talons leaving a long gash down his forehead onto his cheek. Kael regarded the bird with thanks and a low growl erupted from his throat. With swift accuracy, he launched himself at the Captain of the Honor Guard. All that he had within he called upon to assault this animal. To save his sister, avenge his mother; the rage was uncontrolled. A flurry of fists and feet, elbows and knees pummeled him. He rolled the captain to the ground; a grunt of pain and surprise escaped the captain's lips as he drove his fist with unbridled hatred into the man's face.

The years of pent up rage exploded, for his mother and now his sister. Over and over and over he struck the man, until the captain stopped moving. His breath roared in and out of his chest, the bloodlust consumed him and held him like a silent lover, beckoning him with its murderous call. He didn't remember pulling the sharpened stick from his pocket, or plunging it into Akakin's heart, but he had. Not once but three times. He slowed and gasped a ragged breath. He looked at the terror in the man's eyes; the captain's words gurgled in his throat. A cry unheard as his heart fought to keep beating under the savage penetration of the stick. Soon the life left his eyes and he lay in the mud much smaller than he'd been only a few moments ago.

A hand on his shoulder renewed the rage, yanking him, pulling him off of the dying captain. He turned to strike, but the shout echoing in his ears cleared his mind.

"Enough! Enough! He's dead!" Calix screamed.

Sparkles danced before his eyes as the horror of what he'd done filled his vision and he gazed on his whimpering sister.

"You go!" a hand shoved him. "Grab

her and get her home! I'll take care of this," Calix yelled.

He gazed toward Zyla who lay curled up in the mud, a keening wail coming from her. With shaking bloody hands, he bent and picked her up, curling her into his chest. He hushed her when she weakly struggled to fight him off.

"It's okay Zyla, I've got you sister," he murmured softly.

He squeezed her closer and let his eyes drift to the body of Captain Akakin, watching the blood swirl into the muddy water where he lay. He cast a pleading agonized glance at Calix, who nodded.

"Just go, take her home," Calix muttered.

Chapter Five

Calix looked down at the body of Akakin and smiled. It surely didn't hurt his feelings none that the cruel overseer lay dead, swimming in a pool of mud, blood and his own filth. In fact, it rather pleased him. He hated the Captain almost as much as he hated Kael and Zyla.

Rubbing his hands together and blowing on them for some heat, he sucked in a deep breath. His eyes narrowed eyeing the body. He bent carefully not to get any blood or mud on himself and rifled through the dead captain's pockets, stealing anything he could before others came. He grasped at the captains pudgy, cold hand and ripped the tight emerald ring from his pinky finger. Rolling it between his own estimating the food this small treasure would bring him. He didn't think the captain would mind; he was after all… dead.

He stood and glanced around nervously, it wouldn't be good if someone saw him robbing the dead man. When he saw no-one around, he shoved what he found into his pockets and grinned. This was working out far better than he could have even imagined. Kael would be arrested, Akakin was dead and Zyla would be sent to the garrison to be used as a slave, placed at the whim of every soldier there. Yes, this pleased him to no end.

With a skip to his step, he sloshed through the mud to Keifer's office. It was time to report the tragic death of Akakin, he would enjoy watching the chaos that would follow.

Kael

Kael placed Zyla on her bed on the floor. Her fearful cries had turned into soft whimpers as she curled herself into a ball, pulling her torn dress around her. Walking over to the woodstove, he was lost in his thoughts, frantically he tried to think as he dipped a rag into the pot of warm water. They had to leave and run as far away from this place as they could get.

What he did… Killing Akakin… That would get both of them arrested. It didn't matter if that pig deserved it, it didn't matter that he broke the law, the courts wouldn't see it that way. All they would see was that a Gray killed a member of the honor guard.

With a trembling hand, he bent over Zyla and began to sponge the blood from her face.

He spoke to her softly, "Zyla, honey, you need to get up and get dressed. We gotta go, sister," he muttered.

He took one look at her face and cringed. Both lips, mashed and split, her nose was already swollen. Her gentle eyes were turning purplish black and swollen to little slits barely able to see through. It tore into his heart savagely; the burning hatred for Akakin and what he'd done renewed a fresh wave of anger. A chill crawled down his spine when the realization of what happened materialized fully in his mind.

What would've happened to her if he hadn't shown up when he did? Would he have killed her? Left her a bloody heap lying in the mud? Fear gripped his heart like a fist, squeezing painfully, making him catch his breath.

"C'mon Zyla, please," he whispered as he pulled her into a sitting position. She nodded her head slightly and struggled to sit straight, her head swimming; a throbbing that grew with any movement.

"Turn around, I'll get dressed," she murmured.

He heard her choke back a sob as she struggled to her feet. While she dressed, Kael rushed around the one room shack, gathering up what little they had, throwing it into a sack. He would take only what he could carry and leave the rest. It dawned on him that he would never again see his home. Not after what he'd done.

A hint of sadness washed over him when he rubbed his hand across a roughly hewn plank of wood that served as their table. His fingers tracing the names of his mother, father, sister and his own carved into it. A longing ache touched his heart. Although shabby, this shack was the only home he'd ever known. He turned when he felt Zyla's warm hand on his shoulder.

"I'm ready brother," she sighed. With a nod, he led her to the back wall where he pulled the wooden slat open. He poked his head out and checked to see if anyone was near. He saw no one and nodded for Zyla to follow.

Calix

Keifer shot up from his chair, knocking it over. He roared in anger as Calix cowered.

"What do you mean the Captain is dead?" he roared angrily.

Calix took a step back, fearing that he'd completely lose it and start throwing punches. Fear curled in his gut and he gazed at his feet. He suddenly wondered about the wisdom of this plan. It wasn't his, but he may pay the price for it.

"Sir, he's dead," Calix stammered. "His body is in the alley way. It was that boy Kael. He attacked and killed him," His voice wavered and trailed off.

He heard Keifer's breath whoosh out explosively. Briefly daring to lift his chin, he glanced at the man and watched him lift the intercom mike.

"Attention!" Keifer barked. "Squad four, assemble in the courtyard immediately!"

Calix stood unmoving and watched him blow by, shoving him roughly with his shoulder as he passed. He yelled for one of the men while wrapping his belt around his waist, securing the implements onto it. He turned back to the area where Calix stood frozen in fear.

"You!" Keifer snapped, his eyes angry slits, "Stay put!" Calix nodded.

Keifer left, slamming the door behind him. Calix remained motionless in the center of the room, unsure if he should move. He could hear the scuffling outside, all the men preparing to leave. When the voices faded in the distance, he let out a breath of relief. His whole body shook with fear of how Keifer would respond when he returned. His mind searched frantically for his next move. He knew Keifer couldn't hurt him but he feared that his temper would drive the man to forget that. Did he dare go to the main hall and use the phone? He stood listening and questioning what he should do for a time.

He needed to call Baylin to report what happened. With Keifer out of the building he thought his chances were good that he wouldn't be noticed. He decided to go for it. He stood taller and sucked in a deep breath before he let himself out of Keifer's office. He crept to the door and saw it was clear and quickly made his way to the foyer where the phone was. It sat atop the reception desk. The hairs stood on his arm as picked it up, he dialed quickly and nervously shifted his weight from foot to foot waiting for it to connect. On the first ring it was picked up without a word but he knew she was listening; he spoke fast.

"Kael murdered Captain Akakin, you've got everything you need now," he said then hung the phone up.

He glanced around before scurrying back to Keifer's office. He felt his shoulders relax when he'd gotten back to the spot where he was told to stay. The job was done. Now it was just a matter of waiting.

Keifer

Keifer looked down at the body of his captain. Fury sizzled through his body, hot and explosive. He stuck his cold hands in his pockets. He breathed in deeply through his nose and considered the scene. He turned and looked at one of the foot soldiers.

"Send three men to Kael's living unit,

bring back that boy; bloody is best," he barked.

The young soldier grimaced and nodded. "You and you, follow me!" The soldier snapped pointing to two others.

Keifer stood silent a moment and watched them move off in a trot toward the east end of the ally. A few moments later, he turned to the remaining soldiers, his face a mask of stone fury.

"Get a stretcher and bring the captain back to the garrison. Deliver him to the medical ward," he commanded.

He gave one last look at the bloodied body before he sloshed through the mud making his way back. His mind seethed with ideas of just how he would make Kael pay for what he'd done. No one went against the Honor Guard. No one!

He cursed, shaking the mud off his feet as he stomped into his office. Calix stood silent, waiting for the man to say something. He removed his jacket and belt, hung it on the rack and sat coolly to remove his boots, replacing the muddy ones with a clean pair. The sharp motions in his silent changing worried Calix, the man was clearly brooding. He shuffled over to his desk that sat in the midst of the room. The boy stood rigid and Keifer found a certain satisfaction in making him sweat. He sat behind the desk and poured himself a drink, taking a long draw on it before he slammed the glass down making Calix jump.

Keifer looked darkly at Calix. "Tell me everything!" he barked as he watched the young man shuffle his feet nervously.

Calix tipped his face up and nervously told Keifer everything he'd witnessed.

"So, you're telling me Captain Akakin was breaking the law by attacking this girl, Zyla?" Keifer hissed dangerously.

Calix swallowed the lump that had formed in his throat and shook his head. "No sir, that is not what I am telling you at all!" he whined, seeing the dangerous glint in Keifer's eyes. He stammered trying to recover, "It was umm… an unprovoked attack by Kael?" He ventured questioningly. "Captain Akakin was just walking the girl home? Ya know, to make sure she got there safely," he lied a little more confidently.

Keifer nodded and swallowed the last of his drink. "That's what I thought," he said, wiping his mouth with his sleeve.

A soft rap on the door took the attention from Calix and drew both their eyes to the guard, who'd pushed through, standing nervously for permission to speak.

"What is it?" Keifer snapped, irritated that he'd been interrupted. His knuckles rapped lightly on the desk, rat-ta-tat, rat-ta-tat.

The sound made Calix clench his teeth in annoyance.

The guard stammered, trying to speak without fear in his voice. "The man... Kael, he's gone, sir."

The guard's hands wrung in nervous expectation after he'd informed Keifer. Even Calix sucked in a breath, waiting. The moments passed like hours waiting for Keifer to explode. The expressions on his face changed from anger to contemplation before he smiled coldly.

"Release the dogs," he said, his voice dangerously soft, "we're gonna go hunting." He wiped his mouth with his sleeve. "We're gonna find him and his sister, they'll both pay for this."

Calix swore he saw the man drool before continuing. Keifer was evil, every bit as evil as Akakin. He enjoyed the suffering of others. He stood carefully listening to the two men but his thoughts drifted to Baylin and his reward.

The guard nodded and grinned. "Yes sir!" he replied, excitement edging his voice.

Calix watched the guard turn and leave, then brought his eyes back to Keifer who sat behind his desk with a smile on his face. The pleasure Keifer found in the thought of a hunt scared Calix. He hoped he'd never be one of the hunted.

"Sir?" Calix asked.

"Leave but stick around. You'll be needed as a witness once we catch them" Keifer replied, dismissing him.

Calix nodded. "Absolutely sir," he replied.

Kael

Kael dragged his sister along by her hand, his heart raced in terror as they followed the mud rut deep into the woods. His mind was a mess of jumbled, panicked thoughts. His chest burned and from behind he could hear Zyla's breath rasping as she labored to keep up. They reached the meeting spot that he and Mischa had agreed upon so long ago. He let go of Zyla's hand and bent, placing his hands on his knees. Gasping, he struggled to catch his breath.

The sun overhead was just lowering below the tree line, casting the forest into uneasy shadows. He looked around, and back at the way they'd came before he straightened and blew out two whistles, one short, one long. He glanced at Zyla and concern flooded the moment at the sight of her. Her face had blanched to a sickly paleness as she leaned weakly against a tree for support.

She turned her eyes to him. Gasping as

she spoke, "Kael, I can't run anymore," she moaned.

He shook his head. "You'll have to. If we stop now, they'll surely find us," he muttered.

He cringed when he saw tears well up in her eyes. "You shouldn't have done it brother, you shouldn't have killed the captain," she cried softly.

Her face twisted in agony and fear as she sobbed. Kael, hearing the snap of a twig, placed his finger on his lips, motioning for her to be quiet. Her sobs quieted but she couldn't stop them, tears streaming down her battered face she clasped her hand to her mouth. Eyes wide, he peered into the gloom, terrified that they'd been found he scanned the area, straining to peer into the shadows of the fading light. He smiled and released a breath of relief when he saw Mischa step from the shadows.

"Kael? Zyla? What happened?" She said, as she rushed to them.

Kael shook his head in misery and glanced at his sister. Mischa's eyes followed his gaze and she sucked in a hiss when they fell on the battered and fading sight of Zyla.

"Zyla? Oh, my poor baby," she moaned as she moved toward her friend. She pulled her tightly into her arms as if to shield her. She glared at Kael over the top of Zyla's head. "Who did this?" she growled, anger making her voice shake with fury.

"Akakin," Kael replied, glancing away from her accusing stare. He was supposed to protect Zyla, and he had failed.

He heard Mischa crooning softly into Zyla's ear. Questioning the unsaid fear, "Did he?" She asked. He watched Zyla shake her head and Mischa's shoulders drop with relief. She pulled her closer and steadied her.

"I killed him Mischa, I killed him," Kael murmured, still not even believing it himself.

It all seemed like a terrible nightmare. The blinding anger consumed him as he beat him down. Not only for what he'd done to Zyla but for his mother. All the years of suffering his family had endured, the times he wanted to get him and his mother forbade it. He saw it clear as if he were there now, the blood glistening in the sunlight as he plunged the sharpened stick into Akakin's chest.

"We need to run, we need to get Zyla away from here," he moaned.

It shook him to the core when he heard the first excited barks of the dogs. Terror filled his mind and heart. They were too late. With a curse, Kael grabbed Zyla's hand and shot a terrified look at Mischa.

She nodded. "You take her and run south, I'll head north and hopefully the dogs will follow me," she snarled, drawing her knife from its sheath.

Kael shook his head. Those dogs were fast, the best trackers in the country. They would be on Mischa in no time flat. "You can't." He objected.

"Yes! Go! Now!" she snarled as she tore off her scarf and started ripping it into shreds.

Kael, seeing what she'd planned, grabbed Zyla's hand and ran. He would need to trust that Mischa knew what she was doing. His heart pounded in his chest, beating wildly. He ran once again dragging Zyla behind him. He glanced one last time over his shoulder to see Mischa running like the wind through the forest. If she had friends helping her as she'd told him those many times in the past, now would be a valuable time for them to show up.

Dasha, First Rank Keifer

Dasha snarled gleefully as he led the dogs into the forest. He bent down and offered a sniff of a small rag found in the shack. He let them loose to find the trail. The hounds howled excitedly as they stuck their noses to the ground and took off into the woods. Keifer stood behind him with a grin spread wide on his face.

"Okay men spread out!" He barked.

Keifer loved the hunt. There hadn't been on one in a long while. Excitement flowed through his body, energizing him. It worked him to a near frenzy as he followed the dogs and it wasn't long before their braying led him and his men to the first scrap of torn cloth on the ground.

"Okay, we've got the trail," Dasha turned to Keifer. His favorite dog, Kalli, stood beside him pointing. He took the scrap of cloth and held it to her nose. He watched the dog sniff, turn away and return for another sniff then point in another direction.

"What's she doing?" Keifer growled. "Is the stupid dog confused?"

He heard a rumble of laughter come from Dasha. "They've split up. One is headed south, the other north," he said.

Keifer gave him a confused look. "How do you know this?" he asked, sarcasm dripping from his voice.

He didn't like the self-assured pompous ass and found it hard not to let it show. "Because, these rags? They were left purposely to throw the dogs off the trail. But see this?" Dasha asked as he bent low over a bush and pointed to a broken spindly branch, "this is the real direction they are headed," he said softly.

Keifer nodded in understanding. "Okay then, let's get moving," he replied anxiously.

He couldn't wait to get his hands on Kael and that sister of his. Yes, he in fact, looked very forward to it. He'd bring them back alive, but not before he took a bit of retribution from their miserable hides. His fists itched to be used on Kael. And the girl? Well, with Akakin out of the way she was now free game for him. Not that he was really interested in her. He thought her rather homely, too skinny for his taste. He liked his women with a bit more meat on their bones. But, hey, who was he to pass up a freebie? And, to make it even more interesting he had a good mind to make her brother watch while he took her, and perhaps he'd even let his men have a go at her right there after he was through. He was feeling in a generous mood. With a grin he followed behind Dasha.

Kael

Kael's breath roared from his lungs as he heard the dogs moving closer. Panicked, he glanced at Zyla and saw the terror in her eyes. Fear set his heart and mind on fire as he tried to think of a way out of the mess he'd gotten them into. He looked around frantically, seeking some place they could hide. His eyes skimmed over a cross that had been carved into a tree nearby. It was in a curious place, seeing it but not noticing it he continued to scan the area.

"Kael, I'm scared," Zyla whispered.

He nodded. He was scared too. He fleetingly wondered about Mischa. Had they caught her? Was she safe and hiding? His hands shook as he shoved Zyla toward a rocky outcrop.

"Climb, climb sister like your life depends on it," he growled.

He waited until she was about fifty feet up before he started climbing behind her. He watched as she scrambled with her hands and feet, her skinny legs straining to push up toward a cave like depression. He heard them crashing through the woods. He turned and looked behind him and saw the dogs skillfully racing through the trees, dodging branches, jumping over rocks and other debris. He sucked in a deep breath and glanced up at Zyla. She turned to look at him, her eyes imploring him to move faster, her face a mask of horror as the look on his face told her that he would not be following her. She clung to a rock frozen in terror as she watched the first dog leap and grab his ankle.

He shook his head, a cry bursting from his lips. "Keep going Zyla, don't turn around!" he screamed as pain shot through his leg when the dog clamped its teeth into him.

Struggling to shake the dog loose, Kael

kicked out viciously to no avail; the dog was clamped down hard. Laughter rang in his ears as another dog lunged and grabbed him by his arm, the weight of both of them dragging him down. He lay on the ground, panting and screaming. Terror rose in his chest as he watched a shadow move over top of him. In a haze of pain and defeat, he looked up into the cold eyes of First Rank Keifer.

"Oh boy, you sure got yourself in a mess of trouble now didn't you boy?" Keifer crooned as he grinned coldly down into Kael's face.

He didn't see the boot that caught him in the head. He gazed up towards Zyla, a tear rolling down his cheek before the darkness closed in on him.

Zyla

Zyla crouched in the small cave, her breath stuttering in her lungs. She watched from her hiding place as Kael was dragged to the ground by the dogs. Terror forced a scream up her throat but before she could release it, a firm hand clamped over her mouth. Bucking and struggling in absolute terror, she felt an arm snake around her waist.

"Shhhhh...." a man's voice whispered in her ear. Her eyes wild with fear, she craned her neck to see Bevin crouched behind her.

"You can't help him Zyla," he whispered.

Tears filled her eyes and flowed down over her cheeks. Bevin looked firmly at her and placed a finger to his lips to be silent. She nodded and he removed his hand.

She turned to look into his sad eyes. "But he's my brother," she pleaded weakly.

Mischa

Mischa heard the dogs behind her as she ran. She prayed they were following her and not Kael and Zyla. Her knees pumped hard. She pushed herself faster. It was a hopeless exertion and she knew it. The dogs were too close now. A moment of pause and she spotted it. She made a beeline for a boulder and skidded to a halt. She knelt and using her knife she quickly scratched an X onto the boulder's surface. Once it was done she shoved the dagger hard under the soil of the rock. The message would be found. She only prayed that it would be in time to save her. She moved to another large boulder and climbed up beside it and sat cross legged on the ground, melding with the shadows of the setting sun. She couldn't outrun the dogs. She wouldn't even try. The only hope she had was that by giving herself up, it would buy Kael and Zyla the precious time they needed to escape.

Chapter Six

Keifer's fists dripped with blood, Kael's blood. He glanced at the unconscious Kael on the ground and drove his booted foot into the man's ribs, growling. He grew angrier by the minute but knew a better way to make him pay. Kael, no matter how punishing the beating was, would not give up his sister. Keifer glanced at Dasha and the other two soldiers and shook his head in disgust and walked away.

"Grab him and drag his miserable ass back to the garrison!" he ordered without even a glance back.

His knuckles stung and he blew on them with a soft breath, noting the cuts on them from Kael's teeth. They hurt, but he enjoyed it. Beating some little Gray was something that made him feel powerful, and the pain? Well, it was more like a battle wound with some kind of injury to show. Keifer never did any of his own fighting, but liked to feel like a big man by beating up the prisoners. He glanced at them again almost admiring the swelling; he'd have to have the garrison's doctor give him some antibiotic cream to rub onto them. He certainly didn't want to pick up an infection from that piece of trash. He stomped along like the victor of some imagined battle as he made his way back to the main trail.

He'd only gone a few hundred yards when he spied the other scouting party moving toward him. He grinned at the sight of them dragging Mischa between them. Oh, this was turning out better than he could've imagined. Licking his lips, he waited until they were a mere few feet away.

"Mischa my pet, I've been looking for you," he crooned.

She squinted her eyes at him, only a slit was visible in her anger when she glanced up at him. She straightened, her chin jutting defiantly. He laughed huskily before his hand shot out and slapped her hard across the face, rocking her head back.

"Insolent bitch!" he snarled.

Without a word her tongue darted out to lick the bloodied corner of her lip before she smiled up at him. "Oh Keifer," she spoke patronizing in his direction but purposefully avoiding direct eye contact. "Now you know that ain't no way to treat a lady," she hissed at him. Sarcasm dripping from her voice.

A soft snicker from the two men on either side of her escaped and it enraged him. Fury burned in his eyes when he glared at them and they cowered from him and apologized profusely.

She stood defiant smugly smirking at him, driving him to blind rage. The soldiers each glanced at one another and took a step back when they noticed how he stood curling his hand into a fist. He swung hard, knocking her out. Her body lifelessly slumped to the ground and with a huff, he glared at both the foot soldiers daring them to snicker again but neither did.

"Bring her directly to my quarters, I'll take care of this one myself," he growled.

"Yes, sir!" they said in unison. Both men then scrambled to grasp her arms and drag her unconscious body back.

Bevin

Bevin moved slowly through the woods, his steps silent on the carpeted forest floor. He held firmly onto Zyla's hand edging her forward against her fears of returning.

"I'll hide you in my quarters," he said over his shoulder, "at least until I decide what I can do with you." Zyla nodded numbly.

Her thoughts overcome with worry and her heart crushed with pain. Kael was gone. Those soldiers had taken him away. And Mischa… her very best friend in the world, had she been captured too? Tears stung her swollen eyes and rolled down in streaks across her dirty face. She walked slowly behind Bevin. Confused. Why had he saved her? Why was he helping her? She looked at him through new eyes. Before, he'd just been someone who'd requested her services. He hadn't shown any kindness toward her. In fact, he had always appeared aloof and cool. So why now? She couldn't understand what he was doing or why.

Fear tugged at her heart. The questions compounded and took over her thoughts. Was he just tricking her? Was this so that she wouldn't fight him? Was he really bringing her back to imprison her?

As if reading her tumultuous thoughts, she saw him turn and smile warmly at her. "I won't hurt you child," he murmured.

His heart was breaking looking at the terror in her eyes. God, he hated this life. Hated the bowed backs and the shame filled expressions that lined every face in the village. These were his people, the Elitists had enslaved them with this social score. His lineage lead directly back to the first citizen of this village. A lineage that had once been respected. There was no social score then, only hard working people trying to survive. Now his people were thought of as nothing but low class human trash.

His parents watched as the first of their neighbors were taken away for the smallest things, claiming they'd ignored the social score. They'd been the first to take notice of the ugly turn those who thought they were above them all had taken. And how they were fast gaining power. They sent him away to live with his benefactor, Asha. She'd raised him as her own son, giving him her status and her name. Saving him from the life these people were now subjected to live. He swore to her that one day he would intercede. He would fight to change the common laws of social classes.

He'd enlisted in the Honor Guard. Most of the new officers wanted postings in the upper classes but Asha arranged it so that he would be sent here. Under the guise of First Rank, he slowly began to grow the resistance. Many times, he'd pushed to rush that growth, but Asha patiently encouraged him to show restraint. "All the pieces had to come together," she'd admonished him. And she was right. It was with great pain that he restrained himself when he witnessed the beatings, the abuses of the people by the soldiers and commanders. With great restraint he watched as good men died at the hands of the cruelties of the Honor Guard. Anger rose like fire from his chest when he thought of the young boys being shipped to the mines where they would be worked to death by the supervisors to provide coal to warm the elitist's homes. The arena and its great lie. He shook his head and grit his teeth as he thought of it all.

A soft cough behind him reminded him that he had a task to fulfil and returned his focus from his meandering thoughts. He paused and turned, glancing at Zyla. In the tree above her a flutter caught his eye. A lone hawk sat perched on the branch looking down at her. His eyes shifted back to her and the bird vanished. "Curious," he muttered.

His gaze returned to her and in one quick look, he took in her battered face, the slump of her tired shoulders and her expression of defeat. There were still miles to walk through the dark before they would reach his home. With a sigh, he scooped the girl up in his arms, frowning at the lightness of her weight. She was as thin as a waif. His breath caught in the back of his throat when she pressed herself against his chest and curled her arms around his neck. He at once felt hopelessly inept and fiercely protective. Damn that Akakin, damn him to hell! A soft growl passed his lips as he thought of what he'd tried to do to Zyla.

"Sleep child, I'll keep you safe," he murmured as he carried her through the darkness.

Mischa

She woke with her back pressed into the cold wooden floor. Pain rocketed through her jaw. She moaned and placed her hands on either side of her, digging her nails between the slats of wood. The stabbing pain in her head screamed when she pressed forward, pushing herself up to a sitting position.

Through bloodshot and blurry eyes she sat uneasily glancing around the room. She sighed in relief when she recognized it as being Keifer's quarters. Gingerly she touched the swollen area on her jaw, wincing when her fingers grazed it. The man had one hell of a right hook, she'd give him that.

She sat for a moment trying to quell the dizziness in her head before pushing herself to her feet. Yes, this was Keifer's quarters; she recognized the half empty glass ashtray on his bedside stand. She smiled slightly, "I'm in luck."

With an ear tuned in for his footsteps, she tiptoed to his dresser and slid it away from the wall. The screech on the floor sounded like a gong going off inside her head. She grinned thinking of his surprise when he came back and opened the door to an empty room. He had confined her to this room a few too many times in the past, leaving her prisoner in it for hours on end. Nothing to do but search the room and these old Victorian houses... well they were built in a time when secret rooms and passage ways were very much needed. She pressed her hand against a board on the wall and smiled when it turned to reveal a small latch. With a flick of her wrist, the latch opened a crawl space door. It was just big enough for her to slide through.

Once inside, the small space opened to a dark passageway. She hoped she'd never need it again but just in case. She reached back through the door and slid the dresser back against the wall and gently pressed the small door closed; completely covering her hidey hole and enclosing herself in complete darkness. She fished around in her side pocket and with a slight gasp she pulled out a small lighter and a stub of a candle. They hadn't taken it. With the tiny flickering light she crawled her way deeper into the garrison and toward freedom.

Once outside, Mischa squatted beside a large trash dumpster and took a moment to get her bearings. A weak moon overhead flitted in and out of the clouds. What she needed was to get to her shack and grab her weapons. She moved silently in the darkness, with only a glimpse of her between momentary hiding places.

"I hope Kael and Zyla escaped." She sighed to herself. With light, quick steps the silhouette of her shape vanished as she ghosted through the darkness.

Kael

Kael blinked, opening his eyes; they hurt. He gingerly touched the swollen slits and tried to move, but groaned as pain rocked his body. The stone floor of the prison cell bit painfully into his back, the freezing surface stabbed all the way to the bone. He struggled to roll onto his hip and gagged from the blood that ran down the back of his throat. His nose was clogged with dried blood and he sucked air through his mouth greedily. His eyes able to focus more, found a pale glow of light coming through the iron door slat. Tears burned his eyes when it dawned on him where he was and just how serious the trouble he was in.

A disembodied voice from a shadowed corner of the cell startled him. "Boy, you awake?" the voice asked.

"Yes," Kael murmured through his swollen lips.

"Good, I thought those animals had killed you and I ain't keen on being locked in this pit with a dead and rotting corpse if ya know what I mean," the voice murmured.

Kael grimaced, pushing himself up off the floor and into a sitting position. His eyes struggled to adjust to the darkness. "Well, I ain't dead… not yet anyway," he muttered. His lungs screamed in agony every time he took a breath. He figured he had at least a few broken ribs, hopefully that's all it was.

"So, what'd you do to end up here?" the voice asked.

Kael grimaced. His mind wasn't clear yet and he struggled to make sense of everything going on. Should he answer? Should he admit to killing Akakin? What if this person was a spy?

"I killed someone," Kael replied, throwing caution to the wind.

The voice chuckled, "Hope it was someone that needed killing, boy."

"Yup, he did," Kael snapped.

He found it hard to tell if the voice belonged to a man or woman. It had a hushed, gravelly tone. He thought of Akakin and his disgusting hands all over his little sister. The thought of what he'd tried to do turned his stomach. A shuffling noise moved his focus toward the shadowed figure moving up beside him.

"The names Aeryn, pleased to meet you killer," the young man said then grinned shoving his hand out to shake. Kael just nodded not sure he could trust the stranger. He'd seen this man around the village before.

"So why are you here?" Kael asked.

"I got caught stealing," Aeryn replied, a bleak expression shadowing his face. "My baby boy was starving; we needed food! They barely gave us enough to eat." He explained practically pleading for Kael to understand why he stole.

Kael nodded. He knew hunger. It had driven him to steal many times. "I'm sorry," Kael murmured.

Aeryn shook his head. "Don't be, my baby got fed. It was worth the risk."

This too Kael understood. He lowered his head, Kael thought about what would happen to him now. Fear coursed through him, leaving him feeling nauseous. Had Mischa escaped? Was she safe? Where was Zyla? He cringed at the thought of her being in the woods alone, in the dark, or worse yet in the hands of Keifer. Tears slid unchecked down his face. They hadn't run away soon enough. He blamed himself. He knew that Akakin was dogging after her. He should have grabbed her long before this, they should have escaped, got out and ran when he first noticed Akakin's games. But he hadn't dared. Fear and despair kept him from doing what his gut told him he had to do. He had failed… Failed to not only protect his sister but now Mischa will be in trouble now too. Self-loathing burned like a hot coal in his gut.

Anger rose up within and he swiped at the tears. He gazed around the shadowed cell through burning eyes. One lone oil lamp hung high on the stone wall; struggling to cast a pale, yellow glow across the dingy walls of the room. On one wall were two bunks, each covered in a thread bare thin mattress. In the far-right corner a lonely pail stood, barely visible; he suspected it was for the prisoners to relieve themselves.

On shaky legs he groaned when he got up, he stood leaning against the wall to steady himself. Once his head stopped spinning he walked over to it. He bent and lifted the lid on the top of it and gagged when he saw that it was nearly full. He swallowed the urge to vomit and went ahead and added to the vile stench. Every muscle, every bone in his body hurt, and even peeing brought him pain. He replaced the lid on the pail and walked over to the bunks. He looked at Aeryn, really looked at him and sat down on the lower bunk beside him.

"How long have you been here?" he asked.

"Long enough to know I'll never see the light of day again," Aeryn replied in a more cheerful tone than any man sentenced to death might have.

Kael nodded. Yes, most who were sent to prison were never seen again. He suspected Aeryn knew the truth and simply accepted it.

"They're going to kill me aren't they?" he murmured.

Aeryn shrugged his shoulders and glanced sadly at Kael. "I don't know man, I just don't know," he replied.

With that, he moved toward the inner part of the bunk and stretched out, laying back. "You get the top buddy," Aeryn muttered.

Kael raised his face and looked at the top bunk. He didn't think he could climb up to it. Not with the way pain was singing through his body. He nodded to Aeryn, got up and walked over to a shadowed corner, sat down and pressed his back against the wall.

He sighed audibly; this would probably be a very long night.

Chapter Seven

Keifer stood outside the cell door. Shadows danced from the flickering flame of the oil lamp hung on the wall. The hallway smelled of mold, blood, bitter sweat and vomit. His stomach curled in disgust.

He listened quietly. So, the boy admitted to killing the captain. He grinned widely. He had orders from the higher ups that he couldn't kill the little snake, but they said nothing about giving the boy his due. He turned and nodded to the guard. Hands on his hips he fidgeted, waiting, he watched as the guard slipped the key into the lock and opened the cell door. The stench wafted out the door like an evil fog and hit him. He put his hand to his mouth to stifle a gag, this was the worst one yet and it curled his stomach.

"Drag him out, I ain't going into that stench!" he hissed.

The two guards hurried into the cell and grabbed Kael roughly, twisting his arms up behind his back. Keifer grinned when he heard him scream in agony.

"Bring him to the room," he instructed.

The room, a place where he'd tortured many a man and woman was one of his favorite play places. He turned on his heel and stomped away. He'd wait in fresher air for the guards to prepare Kael for the room. He stood outside leaning against the hallway wall picking at his fingernails. He smiled slightly when he heard grunts and cries from Kael as the guards bound his body to the rack. He was getting excited now, he reached over and grabbed a leather strap hanging from the wall outside the door. He lovingly caressed the leather. The smooth gloss of many uses felt like velvet as he ran it over his palm. He stood at the entry, strap hanging from one hand, a glint in his eye that foretold what would happen to Kael. He stepped into the room and shut the door behind him.

"So Kael, we meet again," Keifer crooned softly as he looked into his terrified eyes. He felt a ripple of pleasure rush through him. To be so feared made him feel like a God.

"Where's your sister?" he asked as he slapped the leather strap on his own hand, making the sound of a vicious crack splitting the silence of the room.

"You'll never get her," Kael snarled.

Keifer curled his lips into a sneer. "Oh I think you'll tell me boy," he threatened.

Kael swallowed down hard the fear in his throat that threatened to choke him. Keifer moved around behind him tapping the strap against the edge of the rack. Fear lingered in his anticipation of what this man would do. He couldn't see him but knew he was there, the tapping driving him to near insanity. He gasped when the rough hands of Keifer tore the shirt from his back.

The first lash of the strap flashed like lightening when it ripped the skin on his back. It brought a scream from Kael's lips and Keifer smiled maliciously. He laughed as the boy turned his head and vomited on the floor. His body jumped and writhed to get away from the agonizing pain. The chains that held him at the wrist and ankles, bit into Kael's skin and blood seeped from beneath. Biting over and over the more he struggled against them.

Keifer chuckled as he brought the strap across Kael's back one more time, flaying open his flesh. Another scream rung delightfully in his ears. Kael gasped for breath when he brought the strap down again. He enjoyed this part of his job and liked to remind the prisoners who was boss. He crept up next to his face, bent, his repulsive breath kissing Kael's ear as he whispered softly.

"I'm just getting started boy, so hang on, it's gonna be a wild ride," he chuckled. "You will tell me what I want to know."

Aeryn

Aeryn paced the cell like a caged animal. Kael's screams drifted to his ears and made him cringe. How much more could that poor guy take? He paused feeling anxious, wishing there was something he could do. He glanced at the small cup of water sitting on the floor near his bunk. With a snarl, he tore a strip of cloth from the bottom of his tattered, dirty shirt, forgetting his thirst momentarily. He would use the water to soak the rag and clean Kael's wounds when he returned. They always returned, Keifer liked to make them suffer but if he killed one they would always make him suffer some kind of discipline. That's why he wasn't given the Captain's job. Since then, he always took it right to the edge but never crossed the line. The sound of the strap striking flesh once more made him wince. Another scream echoed in the darkness.

Hours later, Aeryn cringed in the corner when they dragged Kael's unconscious body back into the cell and dropped him unceremoniously midway inside the cell. His lifeless body fell hard onto the floor. A soft moan echoed in the small cell when Kael struggled to consciousness.

Aeryn bent over him and placed a gentle arm beneath him, half carrying, half dragging him to the bunk. He winced when he felt the slick blood from Kael's back soak into the sleeve of his shirt. He didn't know who Kael had killed, but it must've been someone pretty important for him to suffer the beatings Keifer was doling out to him. He'd been there for a bit of time and seen a few come and go, none suffered the abuse Kael did. There was something to this he was sure. He knew he needed to help Kael, even if it were his last act.

Bevin

Bevin laid Zyla carefully on his bed, covering her with a light blanket. Exhaustion kept her asleep and she needed it. Shuffling silently to his dresser, he pulled a phone from inside one of the drawers. Plugging it into the wall, he picked up the receiver and listened for a dial tone. The First Ranks weren't allowed phones, so he kept it well hidden. When he heard the dial tone, he quickly dialed a number that was answered on the first ring.

"They got Kael, but Zyla is safe with me," he said. A heavy sigh filtered through the phone from the other end.

"Okay, get her to safety. I'll figure out how to get Kael out of there," a woman's voice replied.

Bevin grunted. "Asha, they'll kill him, you know that," he muttered.

"Not if I have anything to say about it," she hissed. CLICK! She disconnected without a word more.

He prayed she was right and would be able to stop Kael's death. He returned the phone to its hiding place in the drawer and glanced at Zyla. She was still sleeping soundly. He let himself out into the dark hallway, closing the door silently behind himself. She would be hungry when she woke.

His boots echoed on the wooden floor. He walked with purpose as though he was in a mood all the way to the mess hall. He looked at Odo, the garrison's chef.

"How about a cup of soup Odo? It sure smells good," he cheerfully said.

Odo nodded at him and without a word, turned and ladled out a cup of vegetable soup. Bevin meanwhile grabbed a tray from the rack and helped himself to generous portions of meat and potatoes. He threw on a couple slices of buttered bread.

"Hungry tonight chief?" Odo asked then smiled.

Bevin nodded. "Yeah, chasing bad guys works up the appetite ya know?" he teased.

Odo again nodded. "Well, eat up and come back for more, there's plenty here," Odo replied, waving his arm across the table filled with trays of food.

It was a shame, people in the village were starving and the garrison soldiers ate like pigs at a trough. Odo knew better than to say what was on his thoughts though. That would get him hurt.

"Oh I think this'll be enough for me," Bevin said then laughed as he made a show of hoisting the heavily laden tray.

He grabbed some silverware from the container on his way out of the mess hall and made his way back to his quarters. He looked at the food on his tray and wrinkled his nose. Although he knew Zyla would eat every single morsel, it didn't look nearly as appealing to him.

His mind wandered in and out of the options for these two, barely paying attention to where he was walking. He agonized over it; his face shrouded with worry about how he would get her out of the village. She was too weak to undertake a long and arduous journey to the Badlands, but that was the only place he knew would be far enough outside their reach to hide her. Even the soldiers refused to enter that territory. It was indeed dangerous there, but he suspected not nearly as dangerous as keeping her here. Eventually, someone was sure to discover her hiding in his quarters. If that happened she would be arrested and imprisoned, or worse, he shuddered. Even with his influence he couldn't be sure of what they would do to him if they found her there.

No, the Badlands was his only option. He unlocked the door to his quarters and let himself in, closing the door and leaning against it he sighed.

The Badlands it is.

Chapter Eight

The Darkness

Kael smelled the death on his hands, overwhelming his senses. It was an odor he'd never rid himself of. He bent and grabbed the small body, his thoughts reeling with pain and fury as he looked down on the young girl. Her stomach bloated from starvation; her eyes sunken in a death mask that would never be erased from his mind.

A sharp pain fired through his back when the whip struck him. He sucked in a hiss and gritted his teeth to keep from crying out. The tall stacks of the furnaces sent black smoke high into the sky, blocking out the sun. Ash floated down like ugly gray snowflakes, coating him and everything around him, each breath he sucked it in, choking him.

"Move it or one lash will turn into twenty!" the guard growled; his arm swung wide for another strike to his bowed back. He turned, his eyes flashing with fury, his teeth clamped tightly together. The guard stood before him, the whip dangling from his outstretched arm.

"You want to try me boy?" He hissed at him, eyes narrowed in challenge.

Kael shook his head although

everything in him wanted to rip the man apart. He bowed before him in silent resolution. Slavery, work, hunger, death, all weighed heavily on his shoulders.

How many more bodies were lined up waiting to be thrown into the furnace? He glanced at the pile where others were struggling to stack the dead. He saw faces of those he called friend, faces of those he didn't know. All staring in their masks of death at him, accusing him silently.

Another blow from the whip seared a long line of blood along his back and tears of despair filled his eyes. His head hung. He reached down and grasped the wrists of the next body. A faceless man held the ankles, they heaved the young girl into the incinerator.

Ashes to ashes, dust to dust. He shivered when he felt a tickle from the blood that oozed beneath his shirt, crawling its way to the waistband of his pants. He sank to his knees, bowed his head and tears flowed freely leaving streaks in the ashen gray on his face. Without warning, another strike of the whip curled across his back and the exposed flesh of his neck.

He cried out in pain and desperation tilting his face to the sky.

"On your feet you lazy worm!" the guard roared. A strong and punishing hand grabbed the back of his neck and hauled him upright.

"Move that next body now!" the guard hissed. Kael looked down at the next body and howled in agony. The thin lifeless body lay precarious atop the pile. Wide eyes stared at him in accusation. He begged forgiveness and wept, ignoring the lashing and screams to get the body into the furnace. They all faded, a dull droning in his head as he knelt beside it stroking the long brown hair.

"I'm so sorry," he cried. "I failed you; I promised mother I'd care for you, and I failed."

Zyla's eyes shifted to him and closed.

Kael

Kael's eyes fluttered, the darkness and smell of the cell reminded him of where he was. He gasped in both anguish and relief. Aeryn shuffled beside him, moving something around. Kael turned his head to see him and at the onset of a fiery pain, instantly wished he hadn't. There wasn't a spot on his body that didn't hurt. He felt what little was in his stomach forcing its way up; his jaw tingling with the foreboding of what was about to happen. The pain, already unbearable, couldn't possibly get worse. The involuntary movement of his stomach as it wretched gagged him and he turned his head. Nothing but bile flowed from his mouth. Tears sprang from his bloodshot, puffy eyes and a soft moan bubbled through his swollen lips. The nightmare, real or not would never end. He wondered how much more his body could take before he would finally be released into the silent arms of death.

"Don't move, I've finally gotten your back to stop bleeding," Aeryn snapped at him.

Don't move? Kael didn't think he could move; not even if his life depended on it! His thoughts were flooded with hatred for Keifer. He was the epitome of evil. Everything that was wrong with the world. He was sure to kill him if something didn't change. For him it was like a cat and mouse game. To play with them in some malicious way, watching as they tried to escape or beg for mercy only to be beaten again; to see how much suffering he could cause before releasing his victims to the embrace of death.

The despair that filled Kael's heart was black, a massive cloud of anguish and anxiety. It pushed him further into the blackness, making him want to curl up into a ball, give up and die. His thoughts drifted to Zyla. The way he'd left her hiding on that cliff front, her body tucked into the crevice. He couldn't forget the fear in her eyes and the hopelessness written on her face, when she realized Keifer had won. There was nothing he could do to protect her now. He couldn't, his fate was sealed. Plain and simple, he'd let his temper get the best of him and now it cost him, Zyla, and probably Mischa, their freedom. Zyla would be given over to the garrison as their slave. The thought sent an anguished shiver across his body. Failure tore into him like a rat into a piece of cheese. The dream, etched in his mind; the fears of what her fate would be ripped into his heart.

He cried out, "Zyla, I'm sorry." The tears freely flowing down his cheeks and filling his ears.

His gaze fell to Aeryn. He'd not trusted him, yet this one person washed his wounds and sat over him. He sucked in a deep breath, sniffling up the snot that was building up in his blood filled nostrils. "I'm dying, Aeryn. I don't know how much more I can take," he moaned.

A heavy sigh floated through the darkened cell.

"I know. Someday you will die, but not today my friend," Aeryn replied.

He knew that he was right. Keifer wouldn't let him die today, or probably tomorrow either. He hadn't had his fill of the torture yet. And that would mean more of what he just got… Much more.

"Who in the hell did you kill to warrant such torture?" Aeryn muttered.

Kael squinted into the darkness, his eyes catching the outline of Aeryn's body sitting on the cold floor near the foot of the bunk. It didn't matter much now if he told him, Keifer was going to kill him anyway. At first, he thought Keifer just needed to take out his anger at losing Zyla; but the look in his eyes with every lash said something different. He hated him, truly hated him with every fiber of his soul. Kael had no idea what he'd done to gain such hatred from a man he'd barely ever seen.

"The Captain," Kael said.

"What? You're the one that killed Akakin?" Aeryn spat, rising up to his knees at the edge of the bed.

"He tried to rape my sister. Before I even thought about it, I was on top of him with his blood all over me. He would never get my sister." Kael hissed.

Aeryn gasped. "Man, you fool!" He snapped. "Killing the captain of the honor guard? You might as well have just slit your own throat for all the good it did ya."

Kael nodded. "He won't hurt her now," he sighed.

"No wonder Keifer is drawing this out," Aeryn muttered.

"I'm glad I did it, no matter how much Keifer makes me suffer. I'm glad I did it, he deserved it!" Kael sneered.

He was glad. If he had to do it all over again, he wouldn't even hesitate. It wasn't only to protect Zyla but for all the times he'd beat his mother too. He'd been scared afterwards but also exhilarated. He'd wanted to kill him so bad he could taste it every time his mother would come home bruised and beaten.

"Yeah, but look at you now? Torn up, barely able to move, what were you thinking, Kael?" Aeryn asked. "Was it worth this?"

He turned away from Aeryn. It was. In Kael's heart, he knew his suffering was a price he'd gladly pay to know his sister was safe. At least he hoped she was. He closed his eyes and drifted into an exhausted, heavy sleep.

Keifer

Keifer snarled at the loud ringing. He'd only just returned and hadn't even washed his hands. He reached out and snatched up the phone. He held it to his ear and listened. It never required a "Hello." It was always one of them. He stood listening, gritting his teeth in anger. His fingers curled tightly around the receiver, blood oozing from his recently busted knuckles. An honor guard soldier assigned to be his assistant for the evening stood trembling beside him; never moving, stiff at attention. He didn't dare look away and watched as Keifer's face turned a bright red. He wasn't sure if it was anger or embarrassment. He wasn't stupid enough to ask.

"Yes ma'am, understood!" Keifer barked and then slammed the phone back onto its cradle. His blood pressure began to soar as anger surged through him in a red, blinding haze. He growled, bent and in one wide swipe across the desk sent the phone and everything else crashing to the floor.

"How dare she? How dare that bitch tell me what to do?" He snarled. He glared at the guardsman and turned on his heels and stormed off toward his room.

In his current mood, he almost pitied Mischa who was waiting for him. At least that was something to look forward to, he grinned with a seething malice. He strolled down the hallway and shouted over his shoulder.

"Bring Kael to the infirmary and tell the doc to patch him up and get him ready to travel!" he barked.

He didn't bother acknowledging the man. He knew he would do as he was ordered. Besides, he had better things awaiting him.

He couldn't understand why elitist Baylin would be so interested in Kael. His thoughts surged into paranoia, and he questioned himself. "Who told her about him in the first place?" The words oozed like his own lies he would tell whenever a Gray would die at his hands. He glanced over his shoulder, checking to see if anyone had heard him.

The question of just who'd gone to Baylin chewed at Keifer's mind. "We have a little spy here at the garrison, someone who's reporting everything about the goings on here," he said barely audible. A low growl formed in the back of his throat, he chased these questions around in his mind. His eyes squinting into slits, his arms crossed in front of himself. He stood gazing at the goings on, considering each person. If they had a traitor among them, then he would need to find out who it was. The last thing he needed was any of those Elite, we're-so-better-than-you types, poking around in any of his business here at the garrison. He made a mental note to talk later with Axton, the in-house investigator. Someone was telling tales and he intended to get to the bottom of it.

He unlocked the door to his room and stepped in with a smile on his face. This would take his mind off that hag Baylin. It was time to teach little Miss Mischa a lesson on who was the new boss in town. He paused with the door only cracked open, eyes darting wildly in search of the answer to his thoughts. His face lightened from the scowl and a wide smile emerged. "That's it…She's testing me! I'm to be the new Captain!" With a grin, he flicked the switch on the wall. "Good thing I didn't kill the miserable little maggot."

The pale-yellow light cast the room into a soft glow. He was ready for a grand evening and Mischa was a fiery one. She'd make a fine addition to the captain's private selection. "But not too often, can't have her thinking she is something special." He mused, peering about the room. His eyes widened in surprise when what he found was an empty room.

His roar of anger could be heard echoing into the corridor.

Kael

Rough hands grabbed at Kael, dragging him and throwing him from the top bunk hard onto the stone floor. He screamed in pain when he landed hard enough to knock the wind from him.

Out of the darkness Aeryn shouted, "Leave him alone you animals!"

Someone grabbed him by his hair and hauled him to his feet. His legs were shaking and could barely hold him up, he struggled to stay conscious.

"You're coming with us!" A voice snarled, wrenching his left arm up behind his back. The pain was intense, causing him to lose his breath and sparkles explode in his vision.

"Where, where are you taking me?" he gasped. Terror consumed him when he began to think about going back to the torture room.

"You'll see soon enough," the guard hissed into his ear, his breath stinking against Kael's face. He shoved him toward the door and Kael stumbled, falling on his shoulder and crying out. He couldn't take much more of this, if they were killing him, then just get it over with.

Aeryn sobbed in the background. "Kael?" he moaned.

Kael turned his head and could see the shadow of his cell mate looming in the dark, his stance one that Kael recognized immediately. Not something he'd come to expect from Aeryn.

"Don't, don't," Kael moaned through swollen lips.

Too late! Aeryn launched himself at the guards, filthy pail in hand, he came down hard on the one that had been so rough with Kael. He swung the pail and its filth hitting each of the other two with some form of excrement and the hard side of a pail in a futile attempt to stop them from taking Kael. One of the guards turned and vomited on the floor, retching dry heaves. The one that'd been so rough, obviously the one in charge, pulled his Taser rod and laid it against Aeryn's skin. Kael screamed when he heard the crackle of voltage. He bucked against the guards holding him, thrashed to get loose with a strength he'd thought long gone. He watched unable to help his new friend as the guard, with a grin on his face, drove the Taser rod harder into Aeryn's stomach; his body spasmed and thrashed on the floor. A roar of agony uncurled in Kael's mind as he watched the life leave Aeryn's eyes. The laughter from the guard with the Taser echoing off of the cell walls sent chills down his spine as they dragged him through the door.

"You killed him! You bastards!" Kael screamed. He craned his neck to gaze at Aeryn's lifeless body one last time, a moan of despair escaping his lips.

They laughed. "Did you see that body jerk?"

"Holy shit, I thought his eyeballs were gonna explode," another snorted.

He didn't know where they were taking him, he didn't care. Pain, heart deep, pulled at him and tears ran unchecked down his face. Agony at seeing the friend he'd barely known killed for trying to save him. To these people, to the guards, people like he and Aeryn were nothing, nobody, objects. They showed no pity, no remorse for the things they'd done. His head hung in despair; he just didn't care anymore. He watched the stone tile pass beneath him, the toes of his worn boots dragging across the gaps in the stone. The guards passed the torture room. He looked up and saw the door fall out of his vision. Confused, he watched each door pass until they stopped and turned to another narrow, dark hallway. Through swollen, fevered eyes he numbly stared at the stone floor again, passing beneath him all the same gray; just like him…gray. All hope had fled, leaving only acceptance in its wake. Disembodied voices echoed around him as he was dragged on through one hall after another. Some were anguished moans from other prisoners locked behind steel doors, some laughter as other guards passed by.

Brought to a stop, Kael lifted his head, expecting to see Keifer. Instead they stood in front of a wooden door with a plaque on it that read, Infirmary. Confused, he glanced at the guard on his left.

"What? Gonna have the doc fix me up so Keifer can have another go at me?" he snarled, using the last of his strength to show defiance.

The guard who'd shocked Aeryn smiled, "Dunno boyo, we were told to deliver you here, so that's what we're doing." Then reached out and punched him. It sent a stabbing pain through his ear and into his head making him dizzy.

Before the guard could strike him again, a sharp voice rang out. "Enough!

Guardsman, if I see you strike him one more time, I'll have you busted down to dishwasher!" the angry voice growled.

Kael looked up and saw a tall, thin man standing before him, a man with kind eyes. "Bring him in to the exam room, place him on the table, and do it GENTLY," the man ordered.

Kael watched as the guards turned to leave. He noticed the quiet one paused, stopped, and looked right into his eyes. The man did not have the same look as the others; his eyes were not filled with hate, but sorrow. He tilted his head silently observing him.

He jerked his hands into his pockets and cried out. "Dammit, you guys go on. I have to go back to that shitty cell. I must have dropped my keys in the struggle."

The brutal guard said, "Good! Clean up that mess while you're there." The other one laughed and walked away. The sad eyed guard turned and left without a word.

Kael lay face down on a thin, soft mattress. His bloodied and tattered shirt draped over a chair as the doctor worked on him. Although the doc had given him a pain killer, he still felt every puncture and pull of the needle as each laceration on his back was stitched closed.

"That son of a bitch!" the doc muttered as he drenched another laceration with antibiotic wash before stitching it up.

It seemed like hours to Kael, but in fact, the doctor worked fairly quickly.

"Well boy, you've got three busted ribs, a whole back full of my finest stitching, a broken nose and multiple bruises and scrapes. I've done the best I can. It's up to you now," the doc sighed tiredly.

He stood up, helped Kael roll over and motioned for the nurse. A young man, small and thin, came hurriedly over and reached out to help Kael to a sitting position.

"Hi, I'm Saren," he said.

"Hey," Kael whispered.

"I want him put in room five. Get him some hot soup, a tray of dinner, and load it up… He looks half starved! Also, no one, and I mean no one is allowed to enter his room without my permission!" the doc barked, his gaze turning steely.

The young man nodded, "Yes sir!" he replied then grinned.

After the doc left, the young man came over to sit next to Kael. "I know exactly who the doc meant when he said no-one. The doc meant Keifer and I can't wait to see the look on his face when I deny him access to you."

He got up and shifted a table around so that Kael could reach a water glass. He continued as he cleaned up the bloodied pieces of gauze and put things away. "Would serve him right you know. Ohh, most of us hate the senior officer; hate what he puts the prisoners and civilians through. The man is cruel and heartless." He scoffed. "I'll be right back with some food."

He turned and left locking the door behind himself.

Aeryn

The guard returned to the cell and quickly went to Aeryn. He wasn't breathing. His hands shook as he opened his mouth and blew a large puff of air. He'd tried to move as quickly as he could, guessing about two and half minutes had passed. That's a long time, but before he'd been conscripted to the guard he was studying medical books his grandfather had given him. "Four minutes," he recited. "Must be breathing within four minutes or death." He listened, and nothing. Again, and again he blew air into his lungs, frantically trying to resuscitate the man. Finally, a cough.

Aeryn gasped gulping air into his lungs and choking. He grabbed his stomach in agony with each cough.. His body writhed as he lay gasping for a solid air flow.

"Quickly, we don't have much time." The guardsman said.

"What?" Aeryn groggily coughed with a hoarse voice.

"Dammit, hurry up before someone sees you're alive!" He exclaimed.

Aeryn had no idea what was going on. Half shuffling, half being dragged alongside the man, confusion clouded his thoughts. "Kael?" he looked at the man and asked.

"He's fine." The man grumbled, then looked around a corner. "Shit, this is taking too long."

He shoved Aeryn out a small doorway into the alley behind the garrison. He handed him a piece of paper and a small map. "Quickly, go here. Don't let anyone see you." Aeryn nodded.

"Go quickly, head straight to the place on this map and don't go for your wife and child or you'll be putting them in danger. They'll be ok. That is, as long as everyone thinks you're dead." He looked over his shoulder, "you never saw me... Now go!" He slammed the small door shut.

Chapter Nine

Baylin, a woman of fiftyish, paced in her apartment. Anger curled her hands into fists, and an expression of fury wrinkled her face. "How dare that Keifer overstep his place!"

Well, she'd take care of that problem immediately. She'd be damned if she'd allow him to ruin her plans for that parasite Kael! She smirked when she thought about how Keifer would feel once she'd had him busted back down to foot soldier!

She picked up the phone, dialed and waited for the voice on the other end to pick up. Her eyes gazed down at the street below, the traffic that crawled along at a snail's pace. The city, to her, was beautiful. There were finely cleaned streets; not one scrap of trash on them. Buildings were old but had a Victorian charm and character. Now that spring had arrived, leafy green plants adorned every balcony and stoop bringing pleasant color against the backdrop of wrought iron railings and curtained windows.

She remembered this same street from her childhood, before the Social Score, how dirty and dismal it had been. So many had flocked to the safe zones that the founders couldn't keep up with all of them. Trash overflowed from dumpsters, homeless slept in every alcove and alley way. It was dangerous for a person of quality to even walk the streets without bodyguards. But once the Social Score was introduced, all that changed. The ones with elite scores were able to create the class distinctions and move the undesirable people to the outer zones. They cleaned it up, sure and swift. Laws were made that removed the homeless and sent them away to the villages, where they were relocated into work camps.

As long as Kael and his sister Zyla were allowed to live, then this beautiful city would always be in danger. She wouldn't allow that to happen. It didn't matter if she had to bring down the entire garrison and burn the village. Kael needed to be in the arena! He absolutely must fight! It had to be in the arena and in front of everyone. She had to set an example so that the people would know. He must lose! She'd spent a lot of time and effort finding the right person for him to fight and building the case to put him in the arena with Kael. She hated people who betrayed their own, even if the information was for her. She couldn't leave any witnesses wandering around that would turn on her next.

Keifer could not be allowed to interfere with those plans! She'd planted a seed of discord in that Neanderthal's puny little brain. Now to pull the plug and get rid of both of them, no one would be any wiser.

She bit her lip in regret. A gentle breeze brought the smell of baking bread. She breathed the warm yeasty smell in deeply and sighed, still gazing at the street below. She should have done what she'd originally planned those many years ago, and had both those children killed.

She'd let herself be talked out of it. She'd let herself be swayed by those in higher positions convince her it would lower her own score and possibly move her into one of the lesser zones. Instead of killing them she sent them to live with the Grays… to Rysa where they could be watched. That single decision was now biting them all in the ass. Those two, Zyla and Kael were too dangerous to let live.

Someone had to be protecting the girl, there was no way she could elude them on her own. Baylin made sure they never had enough to eat and that little thing can barely even do decent laundry without tiring. She had Kael, now she just needed the final piece of the puzzle… Zyla.

The voice on the phone startled her. "Brigadier General Thindrel's office, how may I help you Senior Baylin?" the woman's voice asked.

Baylin scowled. She hated the simpering voice on the other end of the phone. "I need to speak to Thindrel, now," she demanded.

The woman sighed. "One moment please," she replied with annoying cheer.

Again she waited. She was becoming frustrated with the time she'd been left on hold. She huffed and motioned for her maid. "Choi, make me a cup of tea."

The light-haired girl nodded in response and hurried from the room.

"Baylin, how can I help you?" Thindrel sighed when he answered. His voice came across as silky smooth as honey, soothing her even as his annoyance ebbed through the line. Baylin turned away from the skulking maid who'd returned with the tea tray and was busily making her a cup.

"I need you to look into a situation for me," she demanded. "One of the Honor Guard has broken several laws concerning the Grays." Her voice, oozing with disdain was ominous.

Again the sigh, "who did what now?" Thindrel asked.

"Keifer, in Rysa," she responded. "I want him removed and penalized for his behavior," Baylin growled.

Thindrel sighed heavily, being more obvious about his lack of interest in her complaint. "What laws has he broken, Baylin?" he asked.

Baylin rolled her eyes in annoyance, she would not be dissuaded. "He damn near killed one of the prisoners, a boy by the name of Kael. I've got reliable information on him abusing prisoners and killing them needlessly. I don't know about you General," she said with dripping sarcasm. "But I think we need the Grays. If Keifer continues killing them needlessly, who will work the mines? Who will continue to work the fields? Although I find the Grays completely distasteful, I also see the need for them and I'm sure you do as well," she hissed. "Perhaps we should start using guardsmen in the arena?" Her voice lowered with a more threatening tone.

"Absolutely, I see what you mean," Thindrel snapped.

He knew Baylin well enough to know she didn't have the Grays best interest in mind, something more was buzzing around in her twisted little mind, but he wouldn't question it. The last thing he needed was to be put in her cross hairs. He wasn't sticking his neck out for some self-important malcontent that got their jollies torturing low scores.

"I'll check into it, Baylin," Thindrel muttered.

He was irritated that once again he was expected to jump because some self-important Elitist got their panties in a twist. Why couldn't they just mind their own business and let the Honor Guard do the jobs they were created to do. So what if a few Grays were killed, in his opinion, the less bottom feeders around, the better.

"See that you do, immediately! I want him busted down to latrine duties by the end of the day." Baylin snapped then slammed the phone back onto its cradle.

She turned into the room and glared at Choi. "My tea?" she asked.

Choi nodded, tendrils of her pinned up hair tickling her face. She then bowed low as a sign of subservience. "Yes ma'am, right here," she said and motioned for the table.

Choi tried to make sense of what she'd overhead. It was only half of the conversation but enough to know Keifer had Kael. She thought this information was something that she should share with Asha. She'd make an excuse later to get out of the house. Shopping for fruit perhaps, Baylin liked fresh oranges for her late afternoon snack. She'd say they needed more. On the way she'd take the route that went by Asha's apartment and slip a note under her door.

Choi thought of her family back in Rysa and her heart ached with sorrow. It was the worst of the worst, many there subsisting off of practically nothing as most of the Gray villages were, but Rysa was the worst. The honor Guard there were sadistic and cruel, using the people of the village as if they were slaves. She hated Baylin and those like her. The Elites who destroyed this once thriving community with their social score.

"Miss Baylin, the almighty, wants her tea," Choi sneered to herself.

Zyla

Zyla woke, the smell of food floating on the air made her mouth water. She opened her eyes in confusion and moaned feebly trying to push herself up in the bed. She looked about the room and recognized it. This was Bevin's bed. Her body hurt. Her face hurt. She remembered Bevin helping her and tears welled up in her eyes. She thought of Kael, she had no idea where they'd taken her brother, or if she'd ever see him again. The panic mounted, she didn't know what would happen to her now. She put her face into her hands and began to sob.

A soft cough from a shadowed corner drew her attention. It was Bevin, "You hungry?" he asked. His voice drifted like a shadow, barely above a whisper.

Zyla nodded.

"Eat then." He motioned to the tray sitting on the bedside stand. "The soup might be a bit cold but it'll do you good."

Zyla's mouth watered at the sight of the food, it was real and not just a dream she'd smelled. Hunger pains tore at her gut. Hesitantly she reached over and grasped the cup of soup. Yes, it was lukewarm but that first taste was exquisite. "mmm…" she muttered, licking her lips. She looked over the rim at him and moved the cup to her mouth again and began chugging it down.

"Whoa, slow down Zyla," Bevin laughed. "You'll get a belly ache if you drink it too fast," he warned.

She lowered the cup and raised her eyes to him and gulped. She saw a gentleness there that almost made her cry again. Other than Kael, not many were kind to her.

"Kael? Have you heard anything about him?" she asked, her voice pleading.

Bevin shook his head. "No, but I'll go see what I can find out, I have some other stuff to do but I didn't want to leave you while you were sleeping," he replied. "I couldn't take the chance you would cry out or try to run."

He'd heard a bit from one of the other guards but he wasn't going to tell her that. The news was too brutal. He doubted Kael would make it through the night with the punishment Keifer was dishing out. He sighed deeply.

"What now? What do I do now? Am I a prisoner?" Zyla murmured, more to herself than to him. With Kael and Mischa gone, she had no one left.

"You're not a prisoner, and I want to keep it that way. We need to get you out of

Rysa," Bevin replied.

He got up from his chair and moved over to sit beside her on the bed. He pulled one of her small hands into his own and looked deep into her eyes.

"I've got a plan, but I need you stronger first."

Zyla nodded, tears flowing down her cheeks.

"I've sent for Mauri, she will help you. You and she have a lot in common, her husband was taken for stealing food for their child," he said.

"Help me with what?" Zyla asked.

"Just to help you get stronger and take care of your wounds. We'll hide out here for a few days, get some decent food into you then we'll have to leave. I want to take you to the Badlands," he explained.

Zyla was startled, her breath caught in her throat and her hand went to her mouth to stifle a yell. She shook her head vehemently.

"The Badlands? Are you insane? That's the most dangerous of all places! Besides that, it is more than five hundred miles away!" She gasped. The terror was chiseled in her face, she couldn't understand how in the hell he could think that she'd be able to undertake a journey that far. She barely had enough strength to put one foot in front of the other.

"I know, I know it sounds scary, but there are people who will help us," he assured her. "You will never be safe here, we can't stay," he said.

She knew she wouldn't, she never was safe in Rysa. The longer she stayed hidden here the more dangerous it would become for both of them.

"But what about Kael and Mischa?" She questioned. "I can't leave them!"

Zyla cried, thinking of her brother and her best friend. Somehow, she needed to find them. Find out if they were okay. Her heart shattered at the thought of escaping and leaving them behind.

"I'll do what I can, Zyla, but I don't know if I can help either of them," he replied honestly.

It would be difficult enough to get her to safety, never mind the other two. A growl of frustration tickled the back of his throat and he wiped a hand across his face, chasing away the fatigue that made his eyes burn with heaviness. If it were possible, he would save everyone from the ravages of the Elites and the Honor Guard, but it wasn't possible, and he wasn't a superman. He could only do his part. They each had a part to play, none ever knowing who or where others in the resistance were. It was safer that way.

Zyla sighed sadly. She knew Bevin was

right. She would never be safe here in the village. If she was caught, her life would be one of pure misery. She just wished she knew where Keifer had taken Kael and then perhaps she could somehow help him. Even if it meant bartering herself for her brother she'd do that… Anything.

She glanced at Bevin and stuffed a piece of bread in her mouth, chewing it slowly. With her mouth full she muttered between chews "Can you try to find out about Kael? Can you help me try to save him?" she pleaded.

"I'll try Zyla but you must know this, you are my main concern. It has to be this way," he replied.

Zyla nodded, confusion clouding her expression. "I don't understand. Why? Why am I so important?" she asked. His determination to save her above the lives of others perplexed her.

"I don't know, I truly don't," he said. "There are those whose orders I follow and they, for whatever reasons, want you safe."

He honestly didn't know. All he knew was that Zyla was important to Asha and he was ordered to keep her safe at all costs. Kael, he knew, would be monitored through Asha, that part of this disaster belonged to her. His part was Zyla. Why either of them was so important to Asha and the resistance was a question that often entered his mind. It didn't matter though, everything she did and everything he did was for the resistance. So, these two… Zyla and Kael must have some important part to play. Otherwise, Asha wouldn't have involved him in this situation and risked his exposure. He gazed at Zyla wondering just what the hell it was that was so special about her and her brother.

Mischa

Mischa moved through the night, stopping briefly at her house to gather whatever she needed. She knew she'd never be back. With a stick she pried up a loose board on the floor and pulled out a leather wrapped package. She let her hands momentarily move over the softness of the leather, let her fingers trace the dragon fly emblem stitched onto the front of it before she opened it. From the package she pulled an old, tattered book. It had dog eared pages and a worn binding where the threads showed through. She held it briefly to her heart before tucking it into the canvas bag slung over her shoulder.

She retrieved other items from the package, a knife, a Taser wand and lastly… a gun. All were prohibited for Grays to possess. She could care less for their laws. She had two goals now. Find and help Kael and then grab Zyla and get them out of the village. She felt sure that Bevin would help her. But getting to him without being seen was a whole different problem. There was no doubt that by now Keifer would have his men out scouring the village looking for her. She thought of what the expression on his face must've been when he found her gone and smirked. "One day," she muttered while packing things. He would one day die by her hand, she vowed.

She stood silent cloaked in darkness, peering out the window into the street. She would stick to the smaller paths back to the garrison. Getting back inside through the secret chamber and crawl space shouldn't be too difficult. She would then need to figure out how to get to Bevin's room.

She had to convince him; alone she wouldn't be able to help either of them. Bevin's help was a must. It was her only hope. With a deep sigh, one that felt like it reached her toes, she slid back out into the night.

It was dark; the crescent moon peeked in and out from behind the clouds. Had there been no clouds it would still be dim, but they helped. Mischa peered out the door, watching momentarily in either direction for movement. She glanced one last time into the small shack, satisfied that the streets were clear she stepped out and quietly shut the door. She skulked through the alley, her slender silhouette barely noticeable flitting from one place of cover to the next.

She was about halfway to the garrison when she saw a small figure walking without a sound. Her hair hung in a long braid alongside her jacket leaping with each nervous glance on either side of her. Mischa crouched low behind a trash pile, rustling a paper in the process.

"Who's there?" The small voice called out. "Show yourself or I'll call for the Honor Guard."

Mischa cringed and made no sound, peering over the pile at the figure. She could easily snatch her and drag her into the small space between the two buildings behind her. She crouched low, waiting… The small figure looked in the other direction and Mischa leapt. She was on her in a flash. Hand across her mouth to stifle the scream. The two figures struggled in the dark, Mischa finally pinning her into the space. She stood panting with her hand around the girl's throat.

The girl's eyes widened, "Mischa?" Her words barely audible with Mischa squeezing her throat a tiny trickle of blood emerged from beneath her fingernail.

Mischa relaxed her grip slightly. She didn't recognize the girl but knew Keifer had people looking for her. "Do I know you?" Mischa hissed through gritted teeth.

The girl's eyes went down leading Mischa to look. Her hands were at her chest, the pointer finger in each hand latched in a crooked X symbol.

Mischa recognized the sign and instantly released her grip. "Don't tell anyone you saw me. I've got to get to the garrison." She whispered.

"Why would you go there?" Mauri asked.

"Shhhh," Mischa hushed. "I've got to try and get to Bevin. My only hope is that he can help me.

"I've been summoned to Bevin's room. Give me a message and I'll bring it to him."

"I don't know." Mischa looked at her suspiciously.

"It's the only way," Mauri said, matter of factly. "Why did you want him?"

"I need him to help me get Zyla."

Mauri looked around, "Shhhh, don't say that name too loud. They've been searching heavily for her."

"They haven't found her?" Mischa asked.

"Not that I've heard." Mauri frowned, "listen, I've got to go. Go to the place in the woods, you'll know it by the…"

Mischa cut her off, "I know, by the

cross in the tree."

"I'll meet you there when I can. Now go!" She demanded. "Get out of the village."

"You'll ask Bevin?" Mischa asked.

"Yes, I'll ask him," she frowned again. "I'll try and see if it will be possible to get his help before I..." she trailed off and began fishing for something inside her coat. She shoved a small pencil into Mischa's hand and grabbed a scrap of paper from the pile Mischa had been hiding behind. "Write it."

"Write it?" Mischa asked.

"I assume you can write?" Mauri snapped.

"Of course I can," she huffed.

"Write what you want. I'm not taking any chances of being sent to the prison if Bevin is not to be trusted. I'll pick it up at the door when I walk in, like it's been slipped under." Mauri looked down and a single tear dropped from her bottom lashes. "They already took my husband, he's probably dead already. Someone has to be around for our child." She sniffed.

Mischa nodded at her and began writing. She shoved the scribbled note into her hand and turned to go. She paused and looked back at her. "Thank you."

Mauri just nodded at her, "Go! I'll leave a note at the marked tree letting you know what he said about the note."

Chapter Ten

Mauri moved quickly, keeping her head low as she walked toward the garrison. Her long unkempt hair hung in dingy strands curtaining her face. Her thoughts churned with many scenarios and questions. It was dangerous for Bevin to call her to the garrison so late in the evening. The law forbade Grays from venturing out after dark. But, she also couldn't disobey his direct command either. Her thoughts went to her son. A two-year-old with his father's eyes. Jorin was a bright and cheerful child; it made her sad to think of what his life would be like. And her husband… Her heart jumped a beat painfully when her thoughts questioned if Aeryn was still alive. She'd had no word and didn't know if he was okay. His arrest made life a little more uneasy, the danger was ever present for her and their son. If any one of the soldiers at the garrison decided to claim her now, she'd have no option but to become their personal property and she'd have no choice. They surely would not allow her to bring Jorin along with her. It didn't matter to them if that left the boy an orphan, they didn't care about such things. She was just a Gray as was the boy and no one would care if they were gone.

Her worries mounted as she walked silently through the muddy streets. She tried to consider how her and Jorin would get by now. Perhaps she could just be like some of the other women who do things for the guard. No, she shook her head in disgust. She had to leave the village and get away before it was too late. If only she knew if Aeryn was alive or dead she would wait for him, he was strong and would be ok in the camps if he survived the arena. She'd heard of others escaping the camps and living in the wilderness, surely he'd return for them. The dream of his return was sweet and made her smile slightly, but he dared not stay too much longer; both her and Jorin's lives were in danger.

As the front porch came into view, she could see the watch guard, a toad of a man, standing guard at the front door. She hesitantly approached with her head low and shoulders hunched, shuffling a few steps closer. He looked down at her, his gaze lazily and brazenly lingering; a sardonic curl to his lips made her shiver. His face was cast in shadows making it look more menacing; the porch lit by a single muted light. She smelled the lingering smoke from a cigarette he'd just extinguished and cast onto the ground alongside the others he'd smoked that night. It didn't matter to him what it looked like, others would come in the morning to clean it up. Grays… the cleanup crew would do it and he cared not for their comforts or needs. But this turn of events might see to some of his. He stepped down a step toward her.

"I've come at the request of First Rank

Bevin," Mauri blurted out hurriedly and lowered her eyes respectably.

A snicker escaped the man's throat and she felt her face flush with the heat of embarrassment. She knew what he was thinking, and it made her angry. She kept her face stoic because she knew better than to show it.

"And why pray tell is the First Rank summoning you this late in the evening?" he said then chuckled.

Mauri seethed with shame and embarrassment, anger and disgust. To the Honor Guard she was nothing more than a cow, to be milked at will.

"I know not sir, I beg of you to please just let me pass," she begged

Her anxiety mounting with every second she had to stand there under his scathing gaze.

He sighed in disgust and stepped aside. "Go, straight to Bevin's chambers! Do not dally," he snapped, swatting her lightly on the shoulder as she stepped passed him.

Everything in her screamed not to shrink away from his touch, she loathed the touch of his filthy hands.

"Thank you Sir," she murmured, trying to choke it out respectably as she walked toward the hallway leading to Bevin's room.

Her shoes, worn and ragged, made soft thudding sounds that echoed lightly as she moved and a breath of relief passed through her lips.

Standing in front of Bevin's door, she bent, slid the note Mischa had given her under the door then waited a few moments before she tapped lightly. The door opened immediately.

"Come in Mauri," Bevin said quickly. Once she'd entered, he stuck his head out the door and looked in either direction to see if anyone had followed her. The hallway was cast in dark shadows, echoing with emptiness. He had hidden Zyla in the bathroom, just in case.

"First Rank Bevin, sir, why did you summon me so late?" Mauri asked quietly.

She squinted looking around the room fidgeting slightly, while letting her eyes adjust to the dim lighting in his quarters. Her hands shook with nervousness and she clenched them into fists at her side, tucking them in the folds of her skirt so he wouldn't see them. In one glance she took in the rumpled bed covers, the empty food tray sitting on the bedside stand and a pair of ratty, torn up shoes slid partially underneath the bed. He already had someone here with him or at least there had been.

She then turned away from the bed and spied the folded paper on the floor that she'd placed there before she knocked. She didn't want him or anyone else to know she'd carried it from Mischa.

"What's that on the floor?" she said. She glanced at him to be sure he'd seen in on the floor by the door before she stooped to pick it up. Standing upright, she immediately handed it to Bevin who looked at it curiously and then back to her before unfolding it.

"I don't know," he said. He refolded the paper and looked up at her, "I can trust you, right Mauri?" he asked, his eyes searching hers.

Mauri nodded. "You know you can, sir," she replied, wondering why the questioning.

His eyes returned to the note in his hand, he turned it over a few times, opened it and read it quickly. A slight smile touched the corner of his mouth as he crumpled it up and shoved it in his pocket.

"I need you to do some things for me." He paused and looked at her sternly. "But, know this… if you get caught, you'll end up in prison." His voice lowered and his eyes squinted, "or worse," he said.

He knew he could trust the woman. They were on the same side; had the same goals and wanted the same things. The only question was if she was up to the task.

"Okay, so tell me why I should risk all this?" Mauri asked.

Instead of telling her, Bevin turned and called out softly. Mauri's eyes followed his gaze.

"You can come out now."

He watched Mauri's face as Zyla crept slowly from behind the bathroom door. He breathed a sigh of relief when he saw Mauri's eyes soften with a gentle expression and a smile form on her lips. His heart warmed and he sighed.

"Oh my God!" She exclaimed. "Zyla, we've been so worried about you child," she cooed at her with her arms wide. She moved toward her and wrapped her into a tight but gentle hug.

Glancing over the top of Zyla's head, she mouthed a silent thank you to Bevin. He nodded with a slight smile. Her eyes glistened with tears as she embraced Zyla who'd begun to sob clinging to her. He could feel the love pouring off of her for the child and knew he'd made the right choice.

"I need your help to get her out of here safely," he said.

Mauri didn't know what he'd planned but she'd do anything she could to help Zyla escape. She'd known Zyla since she was just a toddler. She'd watched her grow through the hardships the Social Score had placed on them all. Although she didn't know why; since she first joined the resistance, she'd been told by others that Zyla and her brother were important and to keep watch on them.

"You've got it, and I'll also tell Mischa she's safe," she replied. She raised her eyebrow and with a nod indicated the note she was not supposed to have known about.

Bevin smiled and relaxed his stance. His expression softened in relief. Things were sure to work out better than he'd hoped. Mischa had escaped, although, he was curious about how she'd managed it; but that would be a question for another day. Zyla was safe for the time being and that was the important thing, and now he could focus on getting her out of the village. She would be ready to travel in a few days, perhaps a week. He wanted the chance to build her strength, get some good food into her. She would still be weak, but she'd manage. He saw steel in Zyla, a toughness, fire that even she didn't know she possessed, at least not yet. Once she was safely out of the village, it would give him time to try and find out more on Kael, if he was even still alive. The thought made him shudder and he gazed at Zyla sitting with Mauri and chatting like schoolgirls. Sadness shadowed his face and he pursed his lips, slightly shaking his head to ward off the thoughts of what Kael must be facing. Asha was his only hope, she was good, but was she that good?

Keifer

The darkness shrouded him as he traveled in the jalopy of a truck to the main headquarters for the Honor Guard located in the central city. The headlights of the truck danced along the trees that lined either side of the road. The craggily shaped limbs seemed to reach for him, creating a surreal feel to the trip. Anxiety welled up inside him, gripping his stomach in a knot. He had no idea why the General had summoned him. But he had a bad feeling about it and suspected it had something to do with his treatment of Kael. Anger rose like bile at the thought of him, the scum sucking Gray. He glanced at the driver who silently steered the truck on its course. He eyed him suspiciously and wondered if the soldier knew anything about this. He was after all the General's personal assistant, he had to know something. He narrowed his eyes, the rage building within and no one to take it out on. Twisting his hands together in nervous anger while the urge to beat the man bloody and get him to spill what he knew seethed deep.

Instead, he pasted a friendly smile on his face. "So, you're the personal assistant to the General, huh? Did he say what this meeting was about?" Keifer asked, trying to school his voice into a modicum of pleasantry. He shoved his hand the man's direction. "The name's Keifer, First Rank Keifer. Yours is?" He asked.

The man pressed his lips together and shook his head. "The name's Ryder sir, and no sir, he doesn't feel the need to confide in me; I'm a mere foot soldier," he replied, his voice dripping with disdain.

He didn't like First Rank Keifer. He'd heard terrible things about this man in the conversations of the General and others. It was hard not to let his feelings show.

"Oh, I'm not worried, just a bit curious," Keifer replied.

The little ass kisser knew alright. He knew why the General wanted to see him; he just wasn't going to tell him. It seemed to him as if this low rank soldier took pleasure in the fact that he was in the dark, so to speak, and was enjoying his discomfort. Well, he'd make sure to take care of this later. He sneered at the man and emitted a barely audible growl.

He wasn't against using his fists on a lower ranking member of the honor guard; in fact, he almost rather enjoyed it when he was given the opportunity. If they stepped out of line or were insubordinate, he'd put them right back in line. This piece of trash, his arrogant attitude, was, in Keifer's opinion, far out of line for his lowly status, refusing to tell a first rank what he asked. Yes, after this meeting was over and they were on their way back to the village… He'd enjoy teaching this boy a lesson he'd not soon forget.

It wasn't long before the vehicle came to a stop in front of the General's quarters. Keifer sat and waited while the soldier got out and walked to his side of the truck, opened the door and stood back at attention. He never flinched in his stance while Keifer lazily got out of the truck.

"Come with me sir," Ryder murmured.

He walked up the four stone steps to the front of the white building. The air was crisp and clear, no heavy, cloying, sooty smell like there was in the village. Keifer breathed in deeply through his nose. The General and those higher up in command lived nice lives here in the city, quite comfortable in fact. Jealousy bit into him. He should be living like this instead of in that dirty little village babysitting the Grays.

Ryder opened the front door and motioned him in. "Wait here please, sir."

He turned and marched down the long hallway and knocked on the very last door. It opened and Keifer could hear murmuring but couldn't make out what was said while he talked to someone in the room.

Keifer's stomach wretched nervously. He had a bad feeling about this whole situation. He sucked in a nervous breath when the man walked toward him.

"The General will be right out. He said to make you comfortable in the study. Can I get you a glass of wine or something hot to drink?" He asked as he steered Keifer toward the General's study.

Keifer shook his head. He just wanted to get this meeting done and over.

"Okay, make yourself comfortable," he said as he exited the room, softly closing the door behind him.

Once gone, Keifer paced, looking around the study. It was covered in dark paneled walls, a massive oak desk sat in the center of the room with the contents on the top neatly arranged. One wall was lined with bookshelves and an endless number of books. In the corner stood a side table with a single decorative lamp that was polished to a shine. Neat, sparse, and cold was the feeling the study gave him. He wondered how anyone could be comfortable in this room.

The door opened and startled him. Keifer scrambled and stood as the General entered. He could tell immediately by the expression on the older man's face that this meeting was going to be anything but pleasant.

Thindrel

Thindrel moved into the room, casting a glance quickly at Keifer. He stood there pathetic, his arm at attention but so out of shape he looked like pile of jelly set in a shirt. He half wanted to make him stay that way but scoffed at him and motioned him to sit. It irritated him that he had to take time out of his schedule to deal with this lowlife sitting in his study. He remembered Keifer when the man first started with the Honor Guard. Remembered how arrogant he was, how he possessed a cruel streak that he'd tried to hide. Thindrel saw it anyway and it bothered him then, the level of cruelty this man possessed was unnerving. Even now, sitting on the chair, well no... sitting was not the right word, perched was a more applicable word. Perched like a bird of prey watching for any sign of weakness, he sat before him with that arrogant expression on his face. It angered Thindrel and he sucked in a deep breath before turning to the First Rank.

"Do you know why you are here?" Thindrel asked calmly.

He calmly poured himself a drink from the pitcher of water that was sitting on the table next to the fireplace. He took a long drink before turning back to him. He was quietly satisfied with the shadow of fear he saw cross Keifer's eyes.

"No sir, I do not sir," Keifer replied, staring straight into the General's eyes trying to maintain his composure.

"We've had complaints about you Keifer, complaints about the dereliction of duties that you were assigned by the Honor Guard," Thindrel replied, his voice low.

Keifer's eyes narrowed to angry slits. "Who sir? Who has complained? Who is spewing these lies about me?" Keifer hissed, barely able to keep his anger under control.

Thindrel raised an eyebrow in warning. "Mind your tone Keifer," he growled.

Keifer swallowed nervously. Thindrel would only be pushed so far with the other man's insolence. "A smarter man would have used discretion in his affairs, but not you, you lack discretion Keifer. Do you know that? You've abused your position and now it's come to bite you in the ass." He turned to his desk rifling with some papers. Silence hung on the air and Keifer was about to speak when he began again. With a sigh he continued, "I was hoping Akakin could've kept you men in line," he snapped. "It's obvious he was just as inept as you and now I have no choice in what has to be done," Thindrel growled, the displeasure of the whole situation written on his face.

"I'm sorry General," Keifer murmured,

lowering his gaze and wringing his hands.

"You've been accused of abusing the prisoners and your guardsmen." He paused and stepped around the desk.

Keifer began to object, but Thindrel cut him off. "The latest report was about a boy by the name of Kael. But he is not the only one is he?" He asked without waiting for an answer. "There were others, other Grays in the village whom are sent for discipline that have also been abused. And… to top it off, you've been accused of murder. What in the hell do you have to say for yourself?" Thindrel asked, shaking his head in disgust.

His disgust was not for those abused or murdered, he could care less about them, they were worthless in his eyes. No, not for them, but in disgust for having to have this distasteful conversation with Keifer.

"I've not abused nor murdered anyone!" Keifer lied.

Images of Kael's bloody back where he took the strap to him just a day ago flitted across his mind and a small tinge of pleasure licked his thoughts. But someone had reported it to the General. Amongst his men a traitor slithered in the shadows. He would find out and when he did, he'd eliminate that problem in the future.

"Do you have proof against me sir?" Keifer asked.

Thindrel's face blanched with anger. "Are you calling me a liar?" Thindrel growled dangerously.

Keifer balked, stuttering his reply. "No, no sir, absolutely not sir," he groveled, "but I am being falsely accused sir."

Thindrel smiled thinly. There was for him just a small amount of pleasure in the task. "I have no choice but to relieve you of your duties at the garrison."

Keifer protested and Thindrel raised his hand for him to be silent. "I've also been ordered to strip you of your rank as a senior officer." He sneered at the now shaking Keifer. He enjoyed the effect it was having on him and continued. "I will be appointing Bevin as the new commander of the Rysa territory," he said smugly and watched a moment for a response.

He turned his back on him, but not before he caught the expression of fury that crossed Keifer's face. Turning back, before Keifer could say anything more, he leaned in and muttered through gritted teeth, "my orders come from those much higher within the social order than me, and I don't relish being this close to their sights," Thindrel said softly. "You are assigned to Ellison Garrison in the south. You will report to commander Zaiden. He's expecting you in the morning. Pack your stuff and get your ass over there," Thindrel ordered.

Keifer began sputtering with indignation and anger. Thindrel turned cold eyes to him. "Enough soldier! You have your orders, now follow them!" he growled.

With a wave of his hand he angrily dismissed Keifer. He was Commander Zaiden's problem now, one he was frankly glad to be rid of.

Keifer

The drive back to the garrison was filled with uneasy silence. Keifer simmered angrily watching the trees pass by. They were not nearly as ominous as they were in the wee hours of the morning. He was being relieved of his duties and relocated to that shithole in the south. He kept that village in shape, kept those over indulged Grays in check. The thought of it was laughable; they'd see when he was gone. That Bevin was soft… He was much too soft for that place. His eyes narrowed when he thought of Ellison garrison. It was worse than Rysa, much worse. It sat on the very edge of the territories. Gritting his teeth he growled, the anger was almost overwhelming. He was barely able keep his anger in check when he glanced at the young assistant to the General. A small smile lifted the corners of his mouth, sarcasm dripping in waves; oozing from his every move. He thought of punching him in his face and wiping that smug expression from his mouth.

His hands shook and he clenched his fists together to keep from striking out. He knew if he did, things would get far worse. His thoughts raced from scenario to scenario, the images of who it would have been danced between the angry images of Kael. He plotted his next move in seething silence. He would find out who turned him in and he would make them pay with their lives. And Kael? Well, that was out of his hands, although, he thought of how one last visit to that boy would be all that was needed to work off his anger. What if he killed him now, what difference would it make? His life was ruined as it was, his career ruined; everything he'd built there was gone. His rank, respect, home, were all gone. Those worthless guards and their simpering Grays would be laughing at him now.

Rage welled up within him as he silently promised himself. 'Yes, people would pay'.

His face affixed in a grimace he stared into the darkness, anger simmering just below the surface. Like a volcano ready to erupt, the fearful rage would escape explosively and burn all those around him. They wouldn't get away with this, he would find out and whoever reported him would know his wrath.

Chapter Eleven

Keifer jumped from the truck before it had even stopped, his hands shook, his whole body trembled with fury, and rage welled up within him. The longer he had to sit next to that sarcastic, arrogant Ryder, the more his temper built. The fury ebbing from every part of him was bringing him to the brink of explosion. His control was nearly gone, almost to a point of no return.

He took the steps two at a time climbing to the entrance of the garrison. He didn't even stop to harass the guard at the door as he normally would. He just pushed past him shoving him aside.

"Sir?" The guard asked.

Keifer paused, turned back squinting at him, pure malice in his eyes. He took two steps closer and punched the guard, knocking him down. Turned on his heel and stormed down the hallway to his quarters. Once inside he stood with his back against the door panting. His stomach growled with hunger. He couldn't believe that he wasn't even offered a meal before he was summarily excused. Anger seethed within him out of control, he lashed out; both arms across the dresser clearing it onto the floor with a loud scream like howl.

He paced furiously grumbling to himself, occasionally shouting. "I'll kill who ever I want!" He shouted this at no one but didn't care amidst his tirade. As tempted as he was to charge down to the prison infirmary, he held himself in check. He wanted to deliver Kael one last hurrah before leaving the garrison and he would, but not before he got himself in a better frame of mind. If he went at him this furiously, he'd kill him too quickly and not have the pleasure of making him suffer. And, oh how he loved making them suffer, he grinned rubbing his hands together. The boy would indeed suffer, that he'd make damn sure of. He needed to get out of his jacket, the sweat was dripping from his brow. He flung it to the floor and threw on a light sweater to cover the fast growing bruises on his arms he'd given himself from terrorizing his room. He wanted food; first order of business, and besides, his thinking was always better with a full stomach.

The hallway leading to the mess hall was quiet, so quiet that he could hear his own footsteps echoing off the walls as he strode through it. In a grand gesture he shoved open the door, made his way to the steam table and picked up a tray. And why shouldn't he? No one knew that he'd been busted down to even less than the cooks. They were on duty round the clock for the convenience of the soldiers, especially those with night duty. Sliding up to the table he glanced up at Odo, who stood at attention, waiting for his food order.

"Give me some of that slop there." He said, pointing at one of vats gently bubbling in a slow simmer.

"Which one, Sir?"

"That one there," he pointed again. "The one that looks like beef stew!" He said leaning forward slamming his hands onto the table and rattling the utensils.

Odo dolloped out a heaping serving nervously handing it over to him. "Boy y'all must be hungry tonight." He said. His giant mitt of a hand grasped the mixing spoon; mindlessly he churned the stew continuing his small talk. "Bevin was just in here a few hours ago. I swear he thinks the food'll run out the way he loaded up his tray."

Keifer was nearly to the door when the last piece of information made him stop and listen.

"He decided to take it back to his room too," Odo said, shaking his head. Never looking up from his pot he continued his musings. A smirk crossed his lips, he continued, "Would seem like I smell bad or something, everyone keeps leaving."

Keifer's eyes shot up at the lower ranking soldier.

"Bevin? Really?" Keifer replied.

Questions arose around what Odo had just said and even Keifer's slow processing began to reveal something out of place. Bevin never took a tray to his room, ever! He always ate in the mess hall, often criticizing those who went against the rule of eating in their quarters. He insisted on setting the proper example, stated as much over and over to Akakin.

Suspicion shrouded Keifer's expression and Odo knew he'd said too much.

Keifer asked him, "what's Bevin up to? Eating in his quarters?"

Odo stood blankly stuttering in search of an answer.

"Is he stealing food to bring to some lowlife Gray? This is the man the General wants to lead the troops, someone who'd sneak food from his own men to feed to those animals," he continued.

Odo's eyebrows raised, he'd never considered that Keifer would not be named as Captain. He was both shocked and terrified that Keifer would do something terrible.

The more Keifer thought about Bevin given the command, the angrier he became. It was supposed to have gone to him, he was the next in line and in his mind, Bevin stole that from him. He glared at Odo and grabbed his tray, storming off toward a table. He sat down shoveling the food into his mouth so fast he didn't even taste it. Keifer knew Bevin was up to something and if he could catch him red handed, then maybe the General would rescind his order and give him the position that so rightly belonged to him.

Odo stood at the serving table watching him, there was no way for him to get out of the mess hall and warn Bevin. Keifer's expression changed with each thought and they grew darker with each passing moment. Bevin was in trouble and there would be no way to stop Keifer. He looked about the empty room for an excuse or another soul to get a message to him but there was no one.

Bevin

Bevin sat on the edge of the bed while Zyla and Mauri sat cross legged on a blanket on the floor. The discussion, planning, had taken far longer than he'd thought it would. He stood, stretching tiredly and yawned. The two women then yawned in unison and giggled.

Bevin noticed how Mauri's eyes kept drifting to the half-eaten tray of food on the bedside stand. She was hungry too. Anger rose within him at the injustice. Damn them who half-starved the people of this little village. His gaze followed hers and he thought of how her little boy was doing, without a doubt he was probably very hungry too.

"So, we're in agreement? Mauri you'll

come twice a day for cleaning and check on Zyla?" Bevin clarified.

Mauri nodded to him. It was a good plan. Zyla needed to get stronger before leaving the garrison. He couldn't be with her and still do his other duties, but also couldn't just leave her alone in the room. Using Mauri as his cleaning woman, no one would question noises from the room and Mauri could take food home to her little one.

He shifted around to the dresser and leaned on it. "Good, by the end of the week, Zyla you will be going with Mauri, she'll take you someplace safe," Bevin said, turning his eyes to hers.

There was a stubborn glint in her eyes as she gazed back at him. "I'm not going anywhere without first finding out about Kael," she growled softly. The set of her shoulders told Bevin to prepare for an argument.

"You have to," he pleaded. "I can't keep you safe here, I can't help your brother if I am worried about you," he hissed.

Mauri nodded in agreement and turned to Zyla. "Honey, Bevin is right, I know you're worried about Kael, we all are. But it won't do you or him any good if you get caught here," Mauri cooed stroking her long dark hair. She was worried about her husband too, but she'd leave him behind if it meant keeping their son safe.

"Find out what you can about Kael, and we'll talk about this tomorrow," Zyla half pleaded, half scowled, hoping to buy a little more time.

She couldn't leave now, at least not without knowing if her brother was dead or alive. And if he was alive where he was. She needed to know what happened after Keifer and the soldiers dragged him off through the woods.

"No, I need answers and if that means marching straight into the prison in broad daylight, then that's what I'll do." She stood and huffed over to the bed and flopped onto it sobbing.

Bevin sighed long and hard, frustrated with Zyla's stubbornness. He shrugged his shoulders and looked to Mauri shaking his head. He was too tired to argue with her.

"Okay Zyla, I'll find out as much as I can, ok?" She sat up and looked at him with tearful red eyes. "I'll take a peek down at the prison, talk to the guards and see what I can find out," he sighed. His face became stern and he continued, "but, I'm warning you, no matter what I find out, you are leaving here at the end of the week, even if I have to carry you kicking and screaming," he growled, glaring at her.

She pressed her lips tightly and

nodded. "Yes sir," she muttered, casting her eyes downward before he could see the flash of defiance in her expression.

"Good, we understand each other then," he grumbled at her because he had seen her defiant look.

He turned to Mauri, who sat silently. His look softened, "before you go, let me get you some food for your little one."

"Thank you, sir," she bowed her head slightly.

"Don't thank me yet, the guards will think I paid you for your service to me," he finished. He was a bit embarrassed by the situation he was putting her in. The guards would think he bedded her and the food was her payment. He loathed how that would tarnish her, it was a horrible thing for him to do to her, but it would also keep her from suspicion. Disgusted with himself for even casting that shadow on her, he also knew that many of the village women whose husbands died were forced to do so to feed their children. The worst part was the expression on her face that should have been outrage was gratitude.

"Give me a few minutes," he spat. He turned and grabbed the dirty tray from the small table and let himself out of the room briefly glancing back to the two women before quietly closing it.

Asha

Asha sat at her writing desk, a soft glow from the lamp casting a soft light across the lined paper. She had to word this perfectly so that if it fell into the wrong hands, no suspicion would be traced back to her. The General had called her, such a ham that he was, and gossiped of the changes in Rysa command. Not that she cared one whit that Akakin was dead. That pig deserved to die. What pleased her was that Bevin was to be in charge.

The General had hoped to gain her favor, telling her all of this. He knew she favored Bevin and hoped that choosing him to replace Keifer whom she despised would impress her. She was pleased and had her servant send him a case of her best Scotch telling him his efforts and demanding work was commendable. Although she knew he had other desires toward her, she never acknowledged it. It was good to have her favor sought after by him. She used it to gain a lot of inside information on the goings on in Rysa. She heard things that she normally wouldn't be privy to. She didn't especially like Thindrel; actually, she found him rather repulsive, but he served a purpose. She finished the note, folded it up and stuffed it into an envelope, sealing it with a wax crest not her own. A simple X indented the blob of wax swiftly hardening on the outer flap. After making certain it was cooled, she summoned her night servant.

"Danika, come quickly girl," she shouted. "I need you to take this to Bacchus. Do not dally," she instructed.

Danika nodded and smiled. "Yes ma'am, right away," she replied.

Asha smiled at the young girl affectionately. Danika had been with her for many years, even through the dark times. They'd grown very close. Although she couldn't openly show her affection when others were around, she lavished her with love when they were alone. Although Danika was her servant, she thought her more of a daughter.

"And Danika, honey, be careful okay?" she warned softly. She hated placing her in danger, but it was important that Bacchus know what was going on.

"Don't worry ma'am, I am always careful," Danika replied, then pecked Asha on the cheek.

With a playful swat, Asha scowled. "You are so fresh sometimes, be mindful of others" she warned and shooed her off.

Danika's soft laughter made her smile momentarily. After she left, Asha sat in the quiet, worrying her lower lip with her teeth. She questioned herself, wondering if should have gotten them out of Rysa sooner. The conflict within her raged and she thought how she should've insisted that they be moved to safety. But she hadn't, and now what a mess there was. The Resistance needed Zyla and Kael. These kids had no idea how important they were. Part of her anguished over the past and what they meant, but the others were right, these two were valuable. She wished she'd taken measures and listened to her own gut instead of waiting. She sat gazing out the window shaking her head wearily. She sighed and turned away pacing, anxious for the return of her girl.

Kael

Consciousness returned slowly. His eyelids felt heavy, barely opening even a sliver no matter how hard he tried to look around. The medication the doctor had given him made him drowsy. He fought the lethargy that made it almost impossible for him to move his limbs. He felt alone in the cold room with a stench of dirt and mold mixed with the smell of solutions the doctors used.

A chair skittered on the floor followed by a soft shuffling of feet alerted him to the presence of someone in the room. He turned to the side and struggled to open his eyes.

"You're waking up I see?" a light, friendly voice said.

Kael nodded; his eyes still unfocused as he glanced around the room. A grunt was all that passed his lips when he'd hoped to ask who was there.

"You're wounds are healing nicely. I've done some perfect knitting on your back boy so no tossing and turning to tear them stitches out okay?" the doctor sternly chided him. "The pain medication will be wearing off soon, you'll be in pain, but I'm only allowed to give you so much." Which was actually none for the prisoners, but it had been ordered for him.

"Orders you know." A slight pause created an awkward silence before he continued, "Those much higher in command don't care if you're in pain, I'm sorry," the doctor explained.

Kael moaned, trying to sit up. A strong but gentle hand pushed him back down. "No, it's too soon for you to try and get up. Let the medicine put you back to sleep for a bit. You're safe for now, rest boy," the doctor said.

Kael nodded weakly. He had no choice but to do what the doctor said. The drugs were still working in his system, no matter how hard he fought to stay awake, he just couldn't seem to hold his eyes open. "Zyla?" he whispered softly. A tear slipped from beneath his closed lid and trickled into his ear.

"She's safe too, now rest," the doctor

murmured and swabbed the moisture.

An expression of pity crossed his face. He didn't for a fact know about Zyla, but he wasn't about to let his patient know that. He prayed if there was indeed a God that he would be looking out for this young man's sister.

Keifer

Keifer had just left the mess hall when he spied Bevin coming down the darkened hallway carrying an empty food tray. Quickly he ducked into the shadows. An expression of anger crossed his face and he clenched his teeth. He hated him. In his twisted mind Bevin had stolen his position and he wondered just what in the hell he was up to. Keifer was crazed with anger and jealousy and once Bevin passed him by, he crept from the shadows and scurried down the hallway. Keifer made his way quietly toward Bevin's quarters. He'd find out once and for all what Bevin was hiding.

For Bevin to be up and about this late at night was unusual. Especially since he knew Bevin was a stickler for early reveille. The man was always up at the crack of dawn, long before any of the other officers, fastidious in his dress and appearance. No, this was suspicious and he would get to the bottom of it. First, he was eating in his quarters, which Keifer knew he was dead set against and now this? Something in his gut told him that Bevin was up to something, hiding something.

The hallway afforded him cover but he paused to check and see if anyone was around. He shook his head in disgust. He should have been watching Bevin more closely. He'd taken him for just a simpleton, one of those who could not change up their habits. He was not worth observation. That was a mistake he was determined to correct because that simpleton just took his job. Stole it right out from under him. He had to know, and began to wonder if he was the traitor. The one to call Thindrel and complain about how he'd been handling things. He thought hard with his twisted perspective and deduced that he'd complained to get his job.

His mind raced from one delusion to the next, he just knew that was it. Something in his gut told him that was how it went and it was Bevin who'd brought this shit show raining down upon him. That was okay, he'd fix him.

With a grin, he stopped in front of Bevin' quarters and listened. A smile lit his face when he heard soft, female voices from behind the closed door. "Well, well, now ain't this a nice surprise," he purred as he slowly turned the doorknob closing the door behind himself.

Stepping fully into the room, he chuckled in surprise to see the two. Zyla was frozen in fear standing near the bed reaching behind her, grasping for anything she could use to defend herself. Mauri, a woman he recognized from the village, stood by the dresser glancing back and forth between Zyla and Keifer, terror keeping her eyes affixed to his every move.

"Well, my night just got a whole lot better," he said softly as his eyes lit on both the women. He turned back to the door and set the lock into place with a soft click. His stomach lurched with excitement and his heart jumped with anticipation as he turned back toward the stunned women, a combination of crazed excitement and rage burning in his eyes.

"Okay ladies, who shall go first?" he teased, a greasy grin spreading on his face, a dangerous glint in his eyes.

He considered the sight before him, and yes, this was going to make all the shit earlier in his night seem so much better. He curled his hands into fists and advanced toward Zyla. She was the one he wanted, he'd deal with other girl later. He smiled a wide toothy grin when he saw Zyla's eyes widen in terror. He enjoyed making others feel fear, it gave him power.

"My, my," he cooed. "First your brother and now you," he said, his voice sickeningly sweet.

He'd intended to follow through with exactly what he had told Kael that he would do to Zyla. Without warning he slung his arm back, and shot his fist out before Zyla even had a chance to dodge the blow. Pleasure coursed through his veins when he felt his fist connect with her soft flesh. Her scream of pain sent a shiver of satisfaction as she crumpled to the floor.

A scream from behind him made him grin even wider when Mauri threw herself against his back lashing at his face and neck with her fingernails. He turned and tossed her off; her slight weight was nothing for him and he carelessly flung her against the wall, shattering the pictures above her head and raining glass shards down on them both. Anger grew and a growl erupted from his throat. He craved this and felt enormous pleasure when he punched her in the stomach, hearing the breath whoosh from her lungs.

"Bitch, you dare to strike me?" he roared. He'd grasped her by her hair, righting her and slapped her across the face. Blood trickled from her split lips, swiftly swelling from his blow. With one swipe of his arm, he sent her flying against the dresser where she crumpled to the floor. His breath heaving with excitement, he turned toward Zyla. Her worst nightmare loomed and suffocated her when he dove on top of her, yanking at her clothes.

"I'm gonna finish what Akakin started

and there's no one to save you this time," he hissed into her ear, ignoring the hitching sobs coming from her. "I made your brother scream like a little girl and I'm gonna make you scream just as much," he laughed. Her meager struggles beneath him only excited him. "What's the matter little one? Are you mad you got your brother killed?" he screamed in her face, his foul breath gagging her just as Akakin's had done.

Bevin

Bevin was returning down the hall when he heard the screams from his room. Terror gripped him and he dropped the tray of food onto the floor, ignoring the clattering. His heart skipped a beat when the fog cleared as to what was happening.

"Keifer." He whispered in a worried panic.

The realization overtook him as he ran, and his breath caught in his throat.

He reached the doorway panting, turned the knob but the door would not open. He heard crashing, whimpers, shouts and screams from behind it. Furiously his hand fumbled with the knob. "Why won't this door open?" He hissed through gritted teeth.

Locked! It's locked. He stood back and

with every ounce of pent up fury, kicked, shattering the lock, the door swinging wide exposing the scene within.

He roared in fury, as one quick glance provided all of the details of the grisly scene unfolding in his room. Mauri lay slumped against the dresser, blood leaking from her nose and mouth, Keifer had Zyla pinned beneath him on the floor, and Bevin could hear her frightened, mewling whimpers as the man tore savagely at her clothing.

Rage, thick and red, filled Bevin's vision consuming all thought. He instinctively launched himself at Keifer. With a growl, he pulled the man from Zyla, throwing him against the wall, knocking over the end table and shattering the clock.

"Keifer!" he growled as he advanced toward him.

Keifer drew his knife from its sheath on his side, and his eyes narrowed. "You would strike a superior officer?" Keifer hissed.

Bevin grinned coldly. "You're not my superior! The call came this afternoon and I'll kill you for this you're now just a worthless low rank; just like the ones you loved to make miserable, I'll do the same for you." he hissed.

Keifer's right eye twitched in his glare at his superior officer. He lunged at him and missed, the light from overhead, glinting off the blade in his hand. With a quick jab, Bevin throat punched Keifer, making him cough and gasp for breath.

A pain shot through his leg when Keifer drove his knife deep into his thigh. Anger and pain rolled together propelled his arm, he back handed Keifer and limped away. He stood a few steps away trying to catch his breath but Keifer came back at him, knife raised, a lone drop of blood dangled at the point of the red tinted blade. Bevin kicked out and knee capped him, causing him to lose his balance and drop the knife, it clattered to the floor. He ignored Keifer's screams of pain and dove at the knife. His fingers latched around the handle of the weapon and in a slow arc, he brought it down through the back of Keifer's neck, severing his spinal cord with a quick flick of his wrist. He watched in stunned horror as the life faded from Keifer's eyes and he collapsed into a crumpled heap on the floor. He knelt, his breath gasping in and out trying to control his racing heart.

Zyla crawled up beside him and wrapped her skinny arms around him, sniffling into his side. He reached around her and pulled her close, protected.

"Oh my God, you killed him," she whimpered. Bevin turned his face to her, his eyes searching hers.

"Did he hurt you?" he moaned.

She shook her head. "No, not that," she

replied, her voice barely a whisper.

He sucked in a deep breath and clenched his hands into fists to keep them from shaking. Swearing, he set her against the bed and made his way to Mauri. His fingers probed and checked for the pulse in her neck. He sighed when he found it strong and steady. He gently lifted her from the floor and she whimpered. His own wound bleeding profusely, he limped over to the bed, laying her gently on it. Blood from the stab wound on his leg soaked the front of his pant leg, drizzling into small puddles where ever he stepped.

"Zyla, I need your help," he muttered weakly. Dizziness buzzed in his head and his vision was getting fuzzy. He stumbled and reached for something to hold himself up. Darkness circled into his vision and breathing deeply through his nose, he sat on the edge of the bed next to Mauri. He felt close to passing out from blood loss but knew he had to stay conscious.

"Close your eyes," Zyla whispered. He did as he was told. The sound of fabric ripping and her firm but gentle hands tying a strip of cloth over his wound bothered him. He opened his eyes and stared into hers.

"Your shirt?" he muttered; his voice thick with faintness.

She nodded and pointed to the bottom

of her shirt. "Don't matter, that pig Keifer already tore it, I just finished the job." Her eyes were cold with hardness.

Bevin glanced around the room. Furniture was strewn everywhere, knocked over and broken, pictures that were once on the walls, now lay scattered across the floor. The dresser stained with a spot of blood from Mauri's head hitting it, and blood pooling on the floor where Keifer now lay in the same position, staring sightlessly at the ceiling.

Bevin put his face into his hands and groaned. "Shit! What have I done?" He looked up at the ceiling and brushed the underside of his chin. "How in the hell am I going to explain this?"

Zyla sat silently watching him, fearful she'd now gotten him in trouble. Just like Kael who saved her from Akakin, would Bevin now be in trouble too?

A single tear ran down her cheek and she hung her head.

A soft cry from behind him on the bed returned him to the situation at hand. He turned to see Mauri staring up at him.

"Is he gone?" she whimpered.

Bevin nodded. "Yeah, he'll never hurt either of you again," he sighed.

Deception

Chapter Twelve

Keifer's body lay motionless on the floor, blood pooling around him. Bevin's face a mask of stunned disbelief, his thoughts dangled on the edge of panic as he struggled to think of what to do about this whole situation. Glancing at Zyla and Mauri, he shook his head. Zyla's face, already yellowing with bruises from Akakin, now sported an eye that was quickly swelling shut, a busted lip that trickled blood down her small chin, and clothing that was ripped askew. Mauri, sat with her head in her hands, trying to stem the flow of blood from a gash on her head.

"We've got to get you both out of here," Bevin murmured, more to himself than them. He stood and paced the room, searching frantically for a solution; for a way to sneak them past the few night guards and out into the village where Mauri could find a hiding spot until morning. A soft cough from Mauri drew his attention.

"I can get her out. I know a way," she said.

Bevin could see the pain in her face and wondered if she might have a concussion.

"You're in no shape I think to go anywhere right now." He turned back towards the door to think. "No, I have to figure out how to hide you both," he replied.

She smiled weakly. "Help me over to the bathroom," she said, then struggled to push herself up from the bed as dizziness made her face turn an ashen gray. Quickly Bevin slid his arms around her to steady her. She swayed unsteadily on her feet but righted herself. Zyla moved to the other side of her and grabbed her arm.

Together they made their way to the bathroom door. Nodding her head for them to go into the bathroom, Mauri pointed to the shower stall and the metal soap dish holder that was molded into the ceramic.

"Under there," she said, "if you slide your fingers just under the lip, you'll feel a small latch. Press it hard," she instructed.

Bevin looked back at her with surprise.

"Before this building was a garrison, it belonged to a man named Thomas, who originally built it. It was once the shining pride of the village, a place where important functions were held, where friends, family and community members were always welcomed." She motioned to sit before she continued. "Everyone knew, well everyone that was now a Gray, about the little oddities of Thomas. And one of those oddities was that he delighted in secret passageways, secret small rooms within rooms and his penchant for the game of hide and seek with his own children and the village children. To say that he was deeply loved by the community was an understatement. When the social score began to settle the classes, those of higher status took his home away for the garrison to watch over the village because it was the nicest one. He was very old even then. He could remember the time before, but died shortly thereafter of what they all thought must have been heartbreak. But his secret has remained alive. Many have escaped the garrison with knowledge of these little passages."

Bevin looked to the shower and did as he was told, and moved his fingers under the soap dish holder. He looked back at the girls, his eyes widened in surprise when he felt a small latch, pressed it and heard a click. Pressing on the wall, he gasped when it slid open a few inches.

"What is this?" he asked, turning his face to Mauri.

She smiled sadly. "This is our way out," she replied. "A small legacy from Thomas," she sighed deeply and looked at Zyla. "Stay close to me and stay quiet. The walls are thin, and we don't want anyone hearing us," she instructed.

She looked to Bevin and stepped through the door into the shadows; peering back at him through the small entry. "I'll take her and find Mischa then come back here in the morning. Don't lock this door because I'm not sure if there's a latch inside.

Bevin nodded. "I won't," he replied as he closed the wall and then drew the shower curtain closed.

He stood staring in wonder at the empty bathroom for a few moments. Curious about how many more secrets about this village they were hiding. A sardonic smile curled his lips. He calmly walked to the dresser, pulled the phone from beneath a pile of folded shirts, plugged it in and dialed. Answered on the second ring, he breathed a sigh of relief when he heard Asha's sleepy voice on the other end.

"Asha, we've got trouble," he whispered.

Zyla

Zyla followed closely behind Mauri. Darkness surrounded them, closing in down the narrow passageway. The weak flame of the lit candle stub threw shadows dancing eerily onto the wooden slat walls. In front of her she could hear soft huffs from Mauri as she skillfully moved along. It was almost as if she'd memorized these passages. Her body protested with every step she took. The past week had been hell and the weakness and injuries filled her with misery. She bit hard on her lower lip staving off the sting of tears creeping in behind her eyes; she steeled herself against the hopelessness that filled her heart swiping the tears angrily and setting her jaw in defiance against it.

She had no idea how they could ever escape this life they were born into. A life they did not choose, where the abuses mounted daily, where hearts shattered and never seemed to mend. There was no way they could go on, day after day in this misery. Part of her wished Akakin had killed her. Part of her just wanted this misery to end. And Kael, her beloved brother and protector, her heart was one of those this life had shattered. She could not bear never seeing him again. At barely fifteen, Zyla only had questions, her life experiences, her youth not offering solutions. She wanted her brother and questioned if Keifer had really killed him. How she prayed he had not.

She mindlessly followed in her desperate thoughts and almost bumped into Mauri when she came to a dead stop in front of her. Mauri bent toward a ventilation grate of some kind.

"Okay, I'm gonna poke my head out and see if it's clear for us to go out this way," Mauri whispered.

Zyla nodded. The ventilation grate looked too small for them to squeeze through and she worried that she'd get stuck. Shaking her head, she watched anxiously as Mauri removed the grated plate and softly slid it to the side. Then she lay flat on her stomach and slid her head through the hole.

She pulled herself back in and looked back to Zyla. "Okay, it's clear, I don't see anyone. Now Zyla, I'm going to slide out, you be quick behind me and don't make a sound," Mauri warned, her eyes boring into Zyla's.

Zyla nodded, her heart in her throat thinking of trying to squeeze through the small square hole. The night air hit her in a wave of bone chilling cold and she shivered. To her amazement she fit with room to spare but they were not clear yet. Nervously she looked around, seeing that they had come out of the passageway at the back of the garrison. The woods were a few hundred yards south of them and she followed Mauri quickly toward the tree line. They were ghosts, flitting among the darkest shadows as they ran. Soon Zyla found herself gasping for breath, drawing in deep gusts of air that burned her lungs. She cried silently; her feet numb from the cold and the pounding they were taking. Every part of her shook as she struggled to keep up. Deeper and deeper into the woods they ran, sticks and branches biting at her skin, her heart raced.

The tree stood before them, large and looming against the backdrop of weak moonlight. Mauri leaned against it. Zyla watched her chest rise and fall as she drew in gasping breaths. This was the same tree with the X that Kael had brought her to.

"Why are we stopping?" Zyla panted, looking around the woods nervously.

She looked for pursuers, she wasn't sure if anyone had seen them running. If the guards spied them as they dodged into the forest, they would surely pursue as they'd done when her and Kael ran here. Her heart slammed against her ribs in anticipation of hearing the dogs set loose against them.

Mauri held her finger to her lips and shook her head, motioning for Zyla to be quiet. Zyla nodded in response. Mauri then pursed her lips, sounding off one long whistle followed by two short ones. Zyla gazed at her confused, that was the same thing her brother had done to call in Mischa. Her heart raced with excitement when she realized it was the same as the one Kael had used.

She blurted her questions out to Mauri. "Was Mischa safe and alive after all?" she looked to Mauri her eyes raised in hopeful question.

Mauri frowned and returned her finger to her lips for her to be quiet. Zyla dared not hope only to have her heart dashed if Mischa didn't show. Breathlessly she waited, shuffling her feet on the dried, brown leaves that littered the ground. It took only a moment before she heard a soft whistle in response and her heart leapt with joy. Mischa was alive! She just knew it!

The shadowed figure moved through the woods toward them, she gave a cry of joy and started moving toward the figure but paused when she felt Mauri lay a restraining hand on her arm.

"No, she'll come to us Zyla."

With excitement she could barely contain Zyla nodded. Mauri was right, she needed to be careful. When Mischa stepped into the circle of weak moonlight, Zyla threw herself at her best friend, hugging her tightly.

"Mischa, I thought they had you, I thought you were dead!" Zyla cried quietly.

Mischa laughed, a hard twinkle in her eyes. "No, not dead, Keifer captured me, but I bested him and escaped,"

Pulling away from Zyla, Mischa leveled her gaze at Mauri. "What happened?" she asked.

Mauri shook her head. "We're in trouble I'm afraid, Bevin too," Mauri replied somberly. "He rescued Zyla and was hiding her in his room, that's why he'd summoned me; to help with her. But somehow Keifer found out about us and attacked us when he was out of the room. Bevin killed him," Mauri finished, her eyes filled with worry.

"Damn," Mischa replied as she pressed her lips together tightly in concern. She looked at Zyla noticing how her tiny body slumped tiredly against the tree.

"Honey, you are going to have to travel tonight with me, I'll take you someplace where you can rest." Her heart ached for Zyla, for all of them. Zyla looked as if she didn't have one more step left in her.

"I'm okay, I can keep up," Zyla replied. Although she wondered if she really would be able to. Her legs, her body, shook with fatigue.

Mischa turned back to Mauri. "Are you okay? Do you think you can make it to the cave?" she asked, concerned.

Mauri shook her head. "I won't be going with you two. I can't leave my son behind and I need to know that Bevin is okay. He did this for us Mischa, he risked it all for Zyla and me," she said softly.

Mischa nodded. She understood completely the sacrifices in the past few days that had been made by all of them. The risks they'd taken and the dangers they'd faced.

"Okay," she sighed, "I'll take Zyla, we'll hunker down in the cave tonight and rest, tomorrow we'll start our journey to the Keepers of the Light. I'll meet you back here in two days. Hopefully you'll know more by then," Mischa said.

Zyla shook her head and began to protest. "But Mauri you need to come with us. I have no idea who these Keepers of the Light are, and what about Kael? I can't leave him behind!"

Before she could utter a word of argument, Mischa glared at her. "You need to do what you're told! This has all been for you Zyla! All of this to keep you safe!" she hissed.

Zyla, shocked at her friend's tone, stared at her angrily. Here again people were at risk for her, it upset her and she began to shout. "What do you mean? For me?" forgetting the danger of being heard.

She was sick of people talking over her, about her and not explaining what was going on. First it was Bevin, now Mauri and Mischa. She was lost and confused and didn't know what was going on.

Mischa cut a glance to Mauri, her expression softening. "Honey, I don't have answers. I don't know. All I know is that you and Kael are important to the Resistance. And we are ordered to protect you at all costs. I will tell you about the Keepers of the Light but other than that, I really can't tell you what I don't know myself," she explained.

A wave of even more confusion moved through Zyla as she pondered the situation. She would have to trust that Mischa knew what she was doing. She'd been her friend all her life and she did trust her.

With a sigh she pushed herself away from the tree. "Okay, let's go then," she muttered as she hugged Mauri then stepped away. "You be careful my friend," she said, her voice hitching on unshed tears.

Mauri gave her shoulder a soft squeeze and then turned to Mischa, tears glistening in her eyes. "Promise me, Mischa, promise me that if anything happens you will get to my son and take him away from this horrible life, promise me," she pleaded, her voice cracking with pain.

Zyla felt her own heart breaking at the desperation in Mauri's voice. She glanced at Mischa, who nodded in agreement. "I will, I promise," she replied.

Chapter Thirteen

Bevin stood before the Honor Guard Police investigator. His shoulders tense, his gaze steady. This was an unfortunate and inconvenient situation that he really didn't have time for. The overhead with its single bulb light cast a cold glare upon them both. The table, a wooden structure with a shiny surface was littered with papers. On the far wall stood a single window that gave view of the darkness outside. He wondered about the police investigators that were in his room, becoming concerned that they may have inadvertently found the secret passageway in the bathroom. He sat silently going over things, recounting his steps to make sure he'd gotten rid of every trace of evidence that would point to the women being there. Nervous tension ran through him; sitting there watching the investigator write notes on a piece of paper, glancing at him every few seconds, then shaking his head.

"So Keifer just attacked you?" he asked for the fourth time, his eyes boring into him intensely making him feel as though he could read his thoughts.

Bevin nodded. "Yes, I caught him in my room, he'd busted the door lock and broke in," he replied. "I don't know why. Perhaps, jealousy?"

The investigator shook his head again

then leaned back in his chair, stretching his long legs in front of him and folding his hands together over an ample stomach that bulged against his silver belt buckle. His face revealed his suspicions and the smug look of unearned power hung on his demeanor.

More of his repeated questioning made Bevin want to lash out at him. "And why do you think he broke into your room? What do you suppose he was looking for?" He asked, his eyes narrowing.

Bevin's gaze, unwavering, looked squarely at the inept investigator obviously trying to assert power he didn't actually possess. He leaned in to make his point "sir, for the fifth time, I don't know. The only thing I can think of is revenge, perhaps you knew he was just busted, and I am now Captain?" he replied, keeping his tone flat.

The man looked at him quizzically and nervously stood but still tried to maintain his composure. "I've heard no such thing."

"You will," Bevin sneered.

A knock at the door drew the investigator's attention. "Enter!" he barked.

Bevin watched as a young man entered the room. Visibly nervous he bent low and whispered something to him. Bevin watched intently as his face blanched of color. The investigator nodded to the young man, stood from his chair and turned to Bevin.

"Your free to go," he muttered, a trace of anger in his voice. "You've got friends in high places it seems, and I've been ordered to cease and desist all investigations into First Rank Keifer's death." Furrowing his brow, he continued, "I didn't know about his demotion and transfer… Sir."

"I knew he was not being promoted and that he'd been busted down to insect. It isn't your job to determine a guilt or innocence by rank and we will be looking into this." Bevin replied.

He pursed his lips. "You can go."

"Thank you," He nodded with a halfhearted salute, turned on his heels smartly and marched out of the small interrogation room, sending up a silent thank you to Asha.

Kael woke and the pain in his back racked his body. This time, his eyes didn't feel as heavy and the sleepy fogginess in his mind was gone. A groan escaped him when he pushed himself up from the bed. It took him a moment, but he swung his legs over the side and sat upright. He had no sense of time and no idea how long he'd been asleep. The pain medication that drugged him offered sleep but little rest. He glanced at the barred window and the darkness outside felt eerie. Memories flooded his mind; he remembered where he was, and Aeryn. His last image of him was lying dead on the cell floor as the guards dragged him out. Tears welled up on his bottom lash thinking of Aeryn. He couldn't understand why he'd risked himself to help him. He knew it would only get him killed. His sorrow for the poor soul that would be his friend mounted and hatred poured through him when his thoughts turned to Keifer. All of the misery that man brought down upon them infuriated him. If he survived, he vowed that one day he would kill him.

His vision cleared as well as his mind and he looked around the room. On a table in the far corner he spied a pitcher of water. He stumbled from the bed, launching himself at it. Thirst drove him to desperately pick it up and guzzle the entire contents, slopping drops of the cool water down the front of his nightshirt. The click of the door lock caused him to pause and he looked up awkwardly when Saren entered the room and locked the door behind himself. Kael wiped his mouth with the sleeve of his shirt and set the pitcher down.

"So, you're finally awake?" Saren said warmly, a smile lighting his eyes.

Kael nodded, glancing at the tray of food the nurse held, wiped his mouth and returned to the bed.

"You're hungry I'm sure," Saren said as he pulled a rolling tray table to the bed and set the tray of food upon it.

Although Kael wanted to eat, was

desperate to eat, he knew not to touch the tray unless given permission first. He glanced at Saren uneasily.

"Go ahead," he exclaimed. "I didn't bring it for me boy," Saren quipped.

Ravenous hunger made his hands shake with want, Kael dug into the food. There was more on this tray than he'd seen in many years. Two slices of bread with butter, a big mug of soup, potatoes with something green sprinkled on them, two large slices of beef and a mound of mixed vegetables. It was almost more than Kael could believe.

"You'll be leaving tomorrow," Saren said as Kael shoved a fork full into his mouth.

Kael glanced up at him, a question in his eyes but he never stopped eating.

"I'm sorry Kael, but scuttlebutt is that you're being transferred to the arena prison. You'll be given the chance to fight for your freedom," Saren muttered in disgust.

He'd heard about the arena although he never witnessed the fights. It was said that those who fought and won, would be given a glorious feast and their families would get supplies enough to last a winter; they would still die because they were criminals, but swift and painless. But only if they won. He'd also heard that the entire promise of ease was a lie. No one knew what happened to the winners, as they were never seen again. That was what the Elites wanted everyone to believe and no one questioned it. At least, not out loud.

Kael felt his appetite turn sour at this news and he shoved his half-eaten meal over.

"I'm leaving?" he gasped.

Saren nodded.

"Tomorrow?"

Saren nodded again.

Kael rubbed a shaking hand across his face and his stomach sank with fear. To fight in the arena. He wasn't sure he was ready or if he had trained hard enough. He knew that one day he'd end up there but wasn't sure it was long enough to even have a prayers chance of winning. Images of the last battle in the arena he'd watched when he was a child haunted him. The smell of the blood wafting to his nose, the roar of the crowd wanting more, felt as real as if he'd watched it only yesterday. A chill poured through his entire body.

"Keifer I suppose ordered this right?" Kael asked, bitterness tinging his voice.

Saren shook his head. "I don't know Kael, I don't know who ordered it."

Kael drew in a deep breath and winced when it pulled at the stitches lining his back. "Okay then, to the arena I must go," he replied with a sad acceptance settling in his heart.

He longed to see Zyla again, just once before he was sent away. He longed to know if she was okay and to say goodbye. His heart felt heavy; he looked down and turned his face away from Saren, gazing out the window. His stare never wavered, even when he heard Saren pick up the tray from the table and let himself back out of the room. There was nothing left to say. Nothing left to do to change it. He'd given it his best fight, and nearly died because of it. The social score would claim him as it had his father. It was in fate's hands now; he would die in the arena and Zyla would be left alone in the world. A world dark and full of danger for her. He'd failed.

He let out a great sigh that looked to take all of the will from him, he choked back a sob and lay back down and closed his eyes.

Baylin

The first rays of sunshine were emerging, way too early for Baylin. The jangling of the bedside phone was more than a little annoying and Baylin turned over, muttering a curse, snatching the receiver from its cradle.

Her voice gravely, she growled at whoever dared to disturb her sleep. "This better be important," she hissed.

The first few rays of sunshine crept through the window. The curtains were not drawn tight and it beamed in, causing her to squint. Growing angry with the lack of care that was taken to ensure the curtains were closed would surely be on her list of things to take care of this morning.

Her interest was piqued, she paused to listen and then smiled coldly. "Thank you," she muttered, "Oh and one other thing, General. I need you to send your man out to Rysa. Arrest a Gray by the name of Calix. I want him brought to the arena prison... Today," she ordered then hung up the phone.

She was already up pacing the room. This was turning out even better than she'd hoped. She was becoming excited and hurried to the bed, picked up the silver bell on the bedside stand and shook it, sending a peel of jingles echoing into the hallway. She sat on the edge of the bed and rubbed her hands together as she thought of the day ahead. Everything was in place and it was all working as though it were meant to.

Kael would be arriving tomorrow. Calix would be arrested today and brought straight through to the prison, Keifer was dead, and the last remaining loose end was the girl, Zyla, and she was determined to have her by week's end. Finally, she would no longer have to worry. All the puzzle pieces would be destroyed and there would be no threat to her precious social order.

A small noise caused her to lift her

eyes; she smiled widely when Choi entered the bedroom.

"I'm going out today. Bring me the blue satin top with the matching skirt," she ordered.

Choi obediently bowed her head and backed out of the room.

Chapter Fourteen

Zyla awoke, startled by the unfamiliar surroundings, she jumped. The dark coolness of the cave surrounded her offering both an eerie and safe feeling. She pulled the blanket around her shoulders and sat up with a moan. Every bone, every muscle in her body hurt. She glanced over to Mischa who sat by a small campfire boiling water in a tin pot. Sitting silently, she cast her gaze over the little room they were in. Two pallets on the floor for sleeping. One wall strung with wooden pegs that held various pots and pans. In one dark corner was a bucket of fresh water that seeped down through the rocks above. The room was sparse, cold and damp, but well-hidden deep within the hillside.

"You're awake. Good, have some tea and then we need to get moving."

Mischa smiled at her handing her a tin cup. Zyla gazed at the greenish liquid, sniffed then tentatively took a sip. It was bitter tasting with an undertone of earthiness.

"What is this?" she asked.

Mischa grinned. "Spring is here, and her bounties are plentiful." She beamed with pride and continued, "you are being treated to the first of the spring tea; a little bit of violet flowers, some nettle leaves with a nice touch of dandelion root."

Zyla smiled and took another sip. "This isn't bad tasting, not good either, but rather different." She said looking at the cup and taking another sip. It felt as though the warmth of it could seep into the achiness of her body and offer sweet relief.

Mischa smiled a small smile and turned toward the pallets. "We've got a long walk ahead of us today," she said. Stooping to grab a blanket. She folded it and packed it into her pack and paused for a second. Mischa again smiled and looked at Zyla over her shoulder. "I've got hardtack and some jerky for breakfast later." Her tone cheery, trying to make it sound appetizing.

Hardtack was a staple of the village people. A bit of flour, a bit of salt and water combined to bake into a very hard, flat cracker of sorts. Sometimes if the villagers were lucky and could find them in season, they would add berries but most of the time, they just had them plain.

Zyla stood and tipped the small cup fully back to swallow the last of her tea and handed the cup to Mischa. Mimicking her she folded her blanket and shoved it into the hand sewn carry pack Mischa had given her and slung it over her shoulder. Standing next to the sleeping area she took a moment to survey the small room. Nothing in the room was hers. Not that she ever had much but it was a little sad to her that now she really had nothing.

She sighed and pressed the wrinkles from her clothes with her hands, smoothing them as best she could. "I guess I'm ready," she said.

Not knowing what she was traveling into worried her. Not knowing what happened to Kael or to Bevin or Mauri worried her even more. Turning her eyes to Mischa she sniffed back tears and tried to put on a happy face. After all, she was here with her best friend and she was happy about finding her.

"So, tell me about the Keepers of the Light?" She asked with a small hitch in her voice. She stepped from the dark, dampness of the cave, emerging into the bright sunshine behind Mischa. She filled her lungs with the fresh, clean mountain air. It smelled glorious with a hint of pine and the musty earthen smell that comes after a spring rain. She stood a moment and let her eyes drink in the beauty of the woods around her. It had been so long since she'd breathed air without the sooty smell of wood smoke in it. She smiled sadly when she thought of how much Kael would love this. How he would love the peacefulness of these mountains and the smell of the clean air. Above her a screech made both of them look to the sky. A hawk, her hawk, circled above them.

"An omen," Mischa smiled.

She sighed as Mischa moved up beside

her. She turned to her, a tear in her eye. "Kael would love this."

"Let's walk, I'll tell you all I know my friend," Mischa replied.

Zyla looked down when she felt Mischa's hand curl into her own.

"Come on." She smiled, "things will be better now, you'll see."

Mischa

Mischa strolled along at an easy pace, enjoying the warm sunshine. Zyla's hand snuggled warmly into hers, it wasn't often such a peaceful feeling was offered. She cast an affectionate glance at the young girl. She thought of the mountains moved to keep this little one safe and the many lives risked. She shook her head. It was worth it. She didn't know why Zyla was so important, but she could feel it deep in her heart that Zyla was the answer to everything. She was the secret that would unfold in due time. She took a deep breath and smiled, hoping... Praying it was true and the time had finally come.

As she strolled along, she began to tell Zyla about the Keepers of the Light. "A long time ago, before white men settled here, there were tribes of people that lived in these mountains. They were called Abenaki, or people of the dawn," she began, unfolding the story of the Keepers of the Light for Zyla.

"For hundreds of years they lived peaceful lives in these woods and mountains, hunting, fishing and coexisting with the land. Then the Europeans came, with their diseases that the people of the dawn had no way to fight. And sadly, it nearly wiped them out," Mischa said, "But a few survived to build the tribes back up. They no longer used the name Abenaki because it would bring persecution and they changed the words from People of the Dawn to the Keepers of the Light as they felt their only purpose was to keep the light of the tribe and the lands from being extinguished once again. They blended into the society until the war. It was then that they returned to the woods and have been here ever since." she explained.

Zyla smiled thinking of these mythical people and wondered why she had never heard this story.

"When the social score was set in place and the elite took control, these mountains and deep woods stayed beyond their reach but not their interest. They needed them to hunt and gather wood but little more than that. Too uncivilized, I guess. They are still unaware of the Keepers of the Light." Mischa paused and looked back to her.

Cautioning her she continued, "they've stayed safe and hidden because we are never to speak of them."

"But you're telling me." Zyla said.

"You… will not be returning to Rysa." She turned and snapped at her.

"But, Kael," Zyla looked at her wounded.

"There are others Zyla, others that are trying to find out about him. Like Bevin, there are many. The Keepers of the Light will keep you safe. They are like ghosts, and they move through these woods unseen," Mischa said.

"So how will we find them to help us?" Zyla asked, her curiosity piqued as she glanced around at the thick woods.

"We won't, they'll find us," Mischa replied then smiled.

Zyla frowned. "Do you suppose they know we're here?" she asked.

Mischa nodded. "Yes, they know, and they'll approach us when they feel the time is right," she winked enjoying the mystery and Zyla's curiosity.

Zyla sighed audibly. "So why me? What is so special about me?" she asked.

She'd heard both Mauri and Bevin mention that this was all about her, all because of her and Kael. And now hearing it as well from Mischa made it even more curious.

"I don't know Zyla. Honestly, I would

tell you if I did," she replied, shrugging her shoulders. "All I know is that you are important to the Resistance. You have a role to play and those that know what it is say you must be protected at all costs. You and Kael." She looked away from Zyla. "We failed Kael, we cannot fail you." Her heart gave a tug of sadness thinking of Kael.

She loved him, more than life itself, but she had to leave him to save his sister. She had to have faith in the others. She'd promised him and she would not break it.

"The resistance is real?" Zyla asked. She'd heard rumors but never took it seriously. She just assumed it was some dumb dream used to escape the reality of Rysa.

"Oh yes, they, or I should say we, are very real," Mischa replied. "Kael is part of the resistance as well as Mauri and Bevin. Did you not know that Zyla?" Mischa asked.

Zyla shook her head. It appeared that Kael had many secrets he'd kept from her. She grew angry and stopped beside a tree to catch her breath and her thoughts.

Mischa noted her shift in attitude and felt she needed more than a moment to process what she'd just told her. "We need some breakfast, this is a good place to rest awhile," she said.

She dropped the satchel she was carrying onto the ground and then sat down beside it. She motioned for Zyla to do the same. Zyla had a look of both exhaustion and confusion, she needed a few moments to gather her thoughts and regain her bearing.

"I'm hungry," she said. "How about you?" she asked looking up at Zyla who still hadn't sat down. Noting this but not saying anything she dug through her satchel and pulled out two bars of the hardtack, handing one to Zyla. From a water bottle she poured them each a tin cup of water.

"I feel like my whole life has been a lie," Zyla said sadly, slumping onto the ground in front of Mischa.

Mischa turned to her, smiling a sad smile. "I know this all seems overwhelming Zyla, and you are confused and shocked by all that I've told you," she handed her a small tin cup.

"I am just so lost," Zyla said, tears welling up in her eyes.

Mischa moved closer to her and wrapped an arm around her. "I know. It's hard to understand everything along with all that you've been through this past week, but you'll see, things will work out. All of it is for a bigger purpose. We may not know right now, exactly what that purpose is, but I am sure it will make things better," Mischa said.

Zyla just nodded and stood. Mischa could see some spark of understanding in her look before she turned away from her.

"Don't wander too far, we're safe enough for the moment but these woods aren't exactly friendly," Mischa said.

Zyla looked back at her. "I won't."

"You should relax," she chided. "I think a few moments quick rest would do you some good. Come, sit and rest a moment." Mischa leaned her back and head against the trunk of a tree and closed her eyes.

Zyla watched as a single ray of sunshine filtered down through the canopy of new spring leaves and danced on Mischa's face.

Chapter Fifteen

Bacchus closed his eyes, rolled his shoulders and smiled. It wasn't a pleasant smile but rather one of disgust. His assignment had been handed down and now he would prepare. He thought of Asha, her impish grin, the way softness flowed with each move she made. To say he would die for her wouldn't be a lie. He would. She very rarely set him to task, but when she did, it always involved killing, in his special kind of way. This time, it would be a guard named Marco. It was necessary. In order to get the package out of the arena safely, the guard would have to die.

He reached into a sliding cubby door just above the fireplace mantle and pulled a seven-inch blade from behind it. The gleaming polished steel had serrated edges with a hand-crafted bone handle that fit perfectly in his palm. Alongside it was a tightly tied sharpening strap. Settling into his favorite chair, a flower printed high backed antique he spent a month's wages to procure. He sat comfortably and began to methodically rub the blade along the strap; an easy rhythm setting itself as he let his mind wander. He thought of how long he'd done Asha's bidding and thought of all the times she'd used his unique services and smiled slightly. He'd known her since she was a teenager and always been somewhere in the shadow of her.

It had indeed been many years.

Kael was being held at the garrison in Rysa and he was the package. They used the term for the safety of Asha and others. No one really trusted anyone in this dance of secrets. He was to be moved tomorrow to the arena prison where he would stay until the day of his competition, one that promised to come too soon. Bacchus wouldn't be able to stop him from having to fight in the arena, nor could Asha, but they could make sure he'd come out the winner; or in this case… the loser. They would have to kill him to save him. It was the only way. But, looks can be deceiving and they planned to deceive everyone. What they'd planned would leave everyone believing he was dead. It would be a nasty piece of work but, he would do it.

He spat on the knife blade and once again moved it slowly back and forth across the leather strap, replaying the plan in his head for clarity. In order to sneak Kael's body from the arena, the guard would have to die. It was a fact though that Bacchus wouldn't mind killing the man. He had a reputation for his cruelty. Brutally torturing those who'd been imprisoned there before their fights. Many times he'd stood by and watched as the guard would venture into one of the cells with his barbed whip and beat a contestant bloody. He told everyone it was to weaken the stronger of the contestants in order to make the competition more equal. Bacchus knew better that man enjoyed his sadistic ministrations a bit too much.

A smile touched his lips as he tested his thumb on the blade, drawing a thin bead of blood to the surface of his skin. He wouldn't mind killing the weasel Marco one bit. In fact, he thought he'd enjoy it. He nodded his head agreeing with himself. He'd definitely enjoy this one.

Calix

Calix sat down at the table, looked at the plate of food before him and grinned. Baylin sure came through on her promise. The cupboards in his little shack were filled with groceries, baskets of vegetables and jars of sauces, dried and canned meats. The largest bags of rice and beans he'd ever seen, at least ten pounds. There were some baked goods and sweets, among other foods. With a gluttonous grin he shoveled spoonful after spoonful into his mouth. It sure did pay well to be of service to the Elites. He didn't care that Kael would die, it didn't matter that Zyla, that snotty little bitch, was wandering and probably dead by now in the woods. What mattered was right in front of him. Food, comfort, the pleasure of knowing he'd gotten rid of the two people he hated the most in this little village as well as Akakin all in one big messy scuffle. A loud bang on his door startled him. He couldn't think of who would be knocking at this hour. He shoved away from the table, swearing under his breath, and shuffled his overstuffed body to the door. He answered the door to see two uniformed men standing on his porch. Shock and fear rifled through his body.

"Sir?" he asked as his stomach sank nervously. They were not Honor Guard but rather Police Guard from the city.

"Are you Calix?" one of the police guard asked.

Calix nodded and puffed out his chest. He felt important, after all Baylin had just showered him with all of this for his service. "I am," he boasted.

"Come with us. You're under arrest," the other police guard demanded reaching behind his back and pulling handcuffs from his belt.

His heart slammed in his chest as his eyes darted in a panic around the small shack, looking for an escape. The police guard withdrew the taser rod from his belt and narrowed his eyes.

"I wouldn't even think about it you little Gray scum," he threatened. He hated the Grays and it would suit him just fine to add a little pain to sweeten the job.

Shock and fear simultaneously washed across his face. "There must be some mistake," he exclaimed. "I demand you call Baylin at once."

The guardsman shoved a piece of paper in his face. "The order is signed by Baylin, now turn around."

Calix bowed his head as one of the police guards jerked his arms behind his back roughly and snapped on the metal cuffs. "What am I being arrested for?" Calix whined.

The guard snickered behind him and leaned in close, his foul breath tickling the back of Calix's dirty neck. "For the murder of First Rank Keifer," he hissed.

Calix gasped in horror and jerked his head around to the guard. "I didn't murder anyone."

The guard just grunted and with a rough hand shoved the middle of his back and pushed him toward the police van. He thought about trying to run but knew he wouldn't get far with his hands bound like they were. He couldn't understand how this could be happening and his stomach roiled with nausea. The stark reality of his situation was like a kick to the stomach. It was all it took. He turned his head and lurched, the vomit ejected on to the ground. The guards drew back in disgust. All he could think of was that all the tasty food he'd just eaten had gone to waste.

The realization that he'd been double crossed by Baylin hit him deep in his gut and he choked back the rage. He thought he was valuable to her; an embedded pair of eyes to keep watch. He questioned why she would do that to him. After all he'd done for her, it made no sense. Before he could form another thought, a powerful blow to his back jarred his spine. One of the police guards drove his fist into him and a howl of pain tore from his lips. Gasping he couldn't maintain his balance. Shoved into the back of the police van, his face hit the cold metal floor, smashing his front teeth. Calix cried out and curled himself into a ball to shelter his face from blows that rained down on him. Pain soared through his face, a blow connecting with his eye, blinding him in his agony.

"You murderous little lowlife," the police guard growled as he climbed in behind Calix. "I'll teach you a lesson you'll not ever forget," he hissed.

From the front of the van a roar of laughter echoed from the other police guard. "Be careful there Sargent, we don't want to kill him just yet, we'll save that for the arena."

Calix's blood ran cold when he heard those words. A bitter smirk touched his face when he realized the irony of it all. He'd been set on his course to ruin Kael and now he was also destined to die.

Kael

Kael sat on the bedside chair and penned the letter to his sister. Saren brought him a notepad and a pen from the outer office.

"Please hurry, I am not sure if the guards will let me send this if they find out."

He'd ignored the pitying looks Saren had cast at him. He didn't need or want anyone's pity. He chewed on the end of the pen nodding at him; his thoughts scattered, kept him from forming the words he'd hoped to share with her. He didn't know how to say goodbye to her. Memories flooded his mind; their times of laughter, Zyla's quick and quirky smile, their times of grief and fear ran through his mind. He wasn't even sure she was still alive. He could only hope. He wasn't sure Saren would be able to get the letter to her if she was. All he knew was Saren had promised to try, to try and find her, to try and give the letter to her. It was the best he could do and more than Kael could have hoped for only a few days ago.

The meal, his last meal at the infirmary, sat beside him on the tray table growing cold. It didn't matter, he would eat it cold. Food had lost its taste and appeal to him. He couldn't help but feel like he'd given up. He probably did, but he was tired of the fight, tired of scraping and scratching to eke out a meager survival against impossible odds. The social score had beaten him and others like him down. They would never have a chance. And he was too disheartened to fight against it anymore. Perhaps the fabled resistance would eventually win against it and those on the upper tiers, but he would never know because he knew that he would die in the arena. He wasn't being fatalistic, just realistic. He hadn't had enough food in the past year to maintain his weight, let alone to build up the muscle mass he needed to be strong enough. He hadn't had time enough to train; although he tried, his fighting skills were minimal at best. That was the reality of it. He swallowed this bitter pill with a grimace.

He scratched the pen across the paper, pouring his love, his fears and his hopes onto the page. Tears leaked hotly from his eyes and he brushed them away impatiently. He needed to get this done. Not for his own sake but in hopes that Zyla was still alive. She would have closure.

He thought of the arena, and who his opponent would be. He hoped against hope that he would be quick enough or strong enough to best him; but in the event he wasn't, that his opponent would take mercy and kill him quickly. That was his biggest fear, dying a slow, agonizing death as his father had; just so the crowds watching could satisfy their bloodlust. With a groan, he folded the finished letter and shoved it into the envelope that

Saren had provided.

"Please understand Zyla," he whispered as he sealed the envelope shut.

He handed the note to Saren and turned to the tray of food and began eating his last meal. His eyes stared blankly, looking at nothing but seeing everything.

Chapter Sixteen

Mauri slid into the bathroom through the secret entry and listened behind the closed door. She heard Bevin moving around inside the room. With her fingernail she tapped lightly on the door and waited. She smiled tiredly when he opened it and motioned for her to enter.

"How's Zyla?" he asked, his voice hushed, almost a whisper.

Mauri smiled. "She's safely on her way to the Keepers of the Light," she replied.

She spied a tray of food sitting on the bedside stand and her stomach growled hungrily. She must've caught Bevin right in the middle of his lunch.

"Eat it," Bevin said and motioned toward the tray. "I can get myself more later."

Mauri nodded and sat on the edge of the bed, helping herself to his food. Hunger drove her to eat what was left fast.

"Have you heard anything on Kael?" she asked around a mouthful of food.

Bevin nodded then grimaced. The news was not good. "Yes," he sighed, "I talked to one of the guards who generally has inside info, for a price. He tells me Kael is alive which is good news, but…" he muttered bitterly, "he's being transferred to the arena prison today."

Mauri groaned as her stomach sank at the news. "What are we going to do, Bevin?" she asked, stunned.

He shook his head. "There is not much we can do now. It's out of my hands," he replied.

The frustration was etched on his face. Mauri could sense his anger, his bitterness at the hopelessness of Kael's situation.

"And you?" she asked, her mouth still full of the last bite of bread she'd shoved into it. "Are you in trouble for killing Keifer?" she glanced over to him and picked at the last morsels of crumbs on his lunch tray. She wished there was more, but, she was thankful for what there was.

"No, the investigator pulled me into his office but let me go after questioning me," he replied, not wanting to share how Asha's part in it had affected the outcome.

"So, what now," Mauri asked. "What about Kael? How are we going to help him?"

"Now? Now you take that little boy of yours and you leave," Bevin replied. "You head out, go meet up with Mischa and let her lead you to safety." He got up and paced the room. "You've done enough Mauri, there's nothing more you can do here." He paused at the dresser where the small piece of torn shirt lay crumpled on top. "We got Zyla out, that was our job," he sighed.

Mauri nodded. Her heart broke at the thought of leaving Kael and her husband Aeryn behind. But she knew Aeryn would want their son to be safe. With a sigh, she got up and hugged Bevin tight.

"You take care my friend and be safe," she said, swallowing the tears that clogged the back of her throat.

Her job was done as he had said and now it was time to take care of her little boy and herself. She was ready to leave Rysa; to get away and find a better life for her son. Turning, she moved quietly into the bathroom, throwing one last glance over her shoulder toward Bevin just before entering the small tunnel.

"Thank you," she whispered. She smiled sadly when he nodded and bowed his head.

Zyla

Zyla's feet felt like they were on fire. She'd walked for what seemed to be miles, following Mischa through the forest. They fought against swarms of black flies, bled through tangles of thorny brush and climbed over fallen trees and boulders. When she saw Mischa finally call their hike to a halt, she collapsed with a moan onto the ground. Her stomach burned with hunger, breakfast had been hours ago, and it was well past time for lunch. She was used to being hungry and not having a lunch but she wasn't hiking through the woods. She easily ignored the gnawing pain in her gut but was still amazed at how much the exertion made her hungry.

"How much further?" she panted as she tried to catch her breath.

Mischa shook her head, her own breath heaving in her chest. "They'll find us when they're ready," she reminded Zyla.

She knew they were watching, she could feel eyes on them. What she didn't know was why they weren't making themselves known. Just then, Zyla heard a twig snap and turned her head to the left. She stared off into the distance squinting to see what was out there. Fear constricted her throat because the forest was full of wild animals such as bear, boar and coyote. Those were the three threats that kept her nervously alert as she walked. She spied movement a few yards off, behind a stand of brush and gasped in fear reaching out and grasping Mischa's hand, pulling her up from her seat on the ground.

"What is that?" she whispered as she pointed toward the brush.

Mischa slowly shook her head and pushed Zyla behind her, shielding her with her own body. From her side she withdrew her knife, grasping it tightly in her fist.

"Stay behind me," she whispered.

Zyla nodded, too afraid to move. She peered over Mischa's shoulders gasping as the brush parted and a tall man stepped out from behind it. In one glance she took in his deep blue eyes that burned through her. Her eyebrows rose as she stood gazing at his dark, almost ebony hair, his lean build and broad shoulders. She lifted her gaze to his mouth which was curled in a sardonic smile.

"Mischa, put that pig sticker down," he teased as he walked toward them.

Mischa chuckled at him and sheathed her knife. "Creed, it's about time you found us." She walked casually over to him and gave him a warm hug. Zyla stood mute, watching the two of them. She coughed lightly drawing Mischa's attention.

"Oh sorry," she smiled at him. "Creed this is Zyla, Zyla, meet Creed, the baddest badass I know," Mischa laughed as she lightly punched him on the arm.

Zyla smiled shyly, her stomach strangely uncomfortable all of a sudden. "Pleased to meet you Creed," she said quietly. She lifted her eyes to his and saw the flicker of arrogance glint in them as he appraised her.

"So, you're the famous Zyla…" He said looking her up and down. "My, my," he drawled and then turned back to Mischa, all but dismissing her.

Zyla's face flushed with embarrassment. She wondered what in the heck that was all about. Anger sizzled in her blood as she glanced at Mischa.

"Excuse me, you're kinda rude," Zyla spat toward his back.

He chuckled before he turned back toward her. "Well your grace, forgive me for ruffling your pretty little feathers," he quipped, exaggerating a low bow.

Mischa hissed, "Creed? Be nice, damn it!"

Zyla watched the two of them. Creed turned and smiled at Mischa. "This is me being nice," he replied, cutting a glance at Zyla.

"Then be nicer!" Mischa snapped, her eyes taking in Zyla's embarrassment and discomfort.

Why was Creed treating her like this? Confused she looked at him sternly.

"Never mind, Mischa, you certainly can't expect manners from a savage any more than a pig," Zyla muttered, sarcasm dripping from her voice.

Creed snickered and ignored it. Mischa shook her head in confusion as she glanced between the two of them. Yes, Creed had always been a little rough around the edges, inappropriate at times but she'd never known him to be this rude to anyone. Shrugging her shoulders, she grabbed Zyla's hand.

"Come on honey," she said softly, noting the hurt in Zyla's eyes.

She turned to Creed and squinted her eyes glaring at him. "Lead the way, we're tired and ready to rest," she snapped.

Zyla watched Creed's back, the roll of his shoulders and the confidence of his steps as he moved easily through the forest. His pace was fast, almost too fast for her to keep up but there was no way she'd let him see her falter. She clenched her fists, gritted her teeth and pushed herself harder, her body screaming with fatigue, pain and hunger. Tears stung the back of her eyes, between the anger, fatigue and fear, she felt lost. She angrily brushed them away with the back of her hand and scowled at him. She watched as Mischa kept up easily with Creed's pace and she envied her friend's stamina and strength.

She wasn't paying attention and stumbled almost falling into Mischa when Creed suddenly stopped and held up his hand. He turned and glanced at Mischa, nodding. Mischa grabbed her hand and yanked her roughly behind a stand of brush, motioning for her to stay quiet; her eyes lit with fearful wariness. Zyla's breath felt trapped in her throat as her heart pounded in fear. She watched over Mischa's shoulder, peering through the thick brush at Creed who crouched low, drawing his knife from its sheath. With a swiftness that mesmerized her, he sprung like a lion. His silent leap landed in tackling a greasy, dirty looking man that was crouched and hidden behind a fallen log. Grunts and body blows met her ears and she tried to see what was happening. She swallowed a scream when another man came charging out of the forest toward them.

In horror and amazement, she watched Creed spin and bring his knife across the second man's throat, blood arcing into the air. It was truly a dance of death. Creed lead the men into his blade; quickly, efficiently and deadly. In a matter of moments, the attack was over, and the two men lay on the ground, their blood still pumping from the wounds in spurts as their hearts beat frantically. Zyla stood motionless, shock on her face watching Creed finish them off with a quick twist of his knife in each man's heart. He stood up, sweat glistened off of his flexed muscles and she caught the pure animal savagery glinting in his blue eyes. Emotionless he wiped the bloody blade across the leg of the man's pants.

As though he felt her eyes on him, he turned and glared coldly into her eyes, sending a chill down her spine; her heart raced, and she stammered to say something. "C'mon, we've not got much daylight left," he snapped.

Zyla nodded with wide eyes and fell

into step behind him. Glancing over her shoulder she saw Mischa rifling through the men's satchels and clothing looking for anything they could use. She swallowed a hard lump; the expression of disgust on Mischa's face when her hands came up empty stunned her. Zyla wondered how she could do that. Rifle through a dead man's pockets and not even show any emotion while doing it. This was not the affectionate and loving Mischa she knew, no this woman was a stranger to her. A sinking feeling of foreboding crept over her. Zyla looked away stifling her words with a grunt.

Hours later Zyla sighed in relief when she saw the small village coming into view off in the distance. It was small and unassuming, set against the base of a huge mountain range. She glanced nervously at Mischa whose eyes were wide with wonder. Even she had never seen the village of the Keepers of the Light; nor had she ever been this far north of the territories.

"So, this is home?" Mischa asked Creed.

He stopped, turned and smiled proudly at Mischa. "This is home,"

The only home he'd ever known. Zyla walked close to Mischa and nervously chewed at her lower lip as they moved closer to the village. It looked a lot like Rysa, plain wooden shacks, a muddy dirt main street, but there was a difference in the people. These people were free, and from the curious expressions on their faces as they passed by them, Zyla could also see that they were happy. She was greeted with warm smiles and nods.

Creed led them to a building that sat quietly off to the left of the dirt street by itself. He knocked on the wooden door before removing his shoes. He motioned for Mischa and Zyla to do the same. The door opened and an older woman stood in the doorway gazing at the threesome. If Zyla had to guess, she would estimate she was somewhere around fifty years old. There were not many older people in Rysa, most went to the arena long before then.

"Creed? You're back!" the woman squealed happily pulling him into her arms for a hug.

He chuckled softly trying to maintain his tough exterior while this woman hugged him. "Is grandfather around?" he asked as he pulled himself from the woman's arms.

She smiled and nodded, then glanced at Zyla. "This must be Zyla?" she asked smiling warmly at her.

Zyla felt her face flush with warmth. She wondered how these people knew her.

"Yes, the one and only," Creed drawled dryly.

The woman glanced at him and

frowned. "And Kael? Is he not with you?" she asked, glancing over his shoulder in question.

A small gasp escaped and Zyla's breath caught in the back of her throat at the mention of her brother's name. Mischa slid her hand into hers and gave it a slight squeeze.

"No, Kael didn't make it out," Creed murmured.

The older woman's eyes glistened with tears and she sighed. "Well, welcome Zyla, grandfather will be pleased to see you," the woman gazed at her warmly as she stepped aside and ushered them all in.

Zyla stepped through the door hesitantly. She felt a gentle nudge from Mischa behind her. "Go ahead honey, these people are your friends," Mischa whispered reassuringly.

Zyla drew in a deep breath and stepped into the small room. Her eyes widened as they set on an elderly man sitting in a rocking chair with a blanket draped lazily across his lap. His eyes appeared to fill with immense happiness, beaming with love as he gazed back at her.

"Welcome home Zyla," he said warmly as he smiled.

Zyla's breath caught hitching as she stared at the man. Her eyes transfixed on a man who could have been the identical twin of her own mother.

"Do I know you?" she stuttered.

Soft laughter met her ears. "We are blood my child, so yes, your soul recognizes mine," the old man replied, a joyful lilt singing in his husky voice.

Her head began to spin, darkness circled in on her vision bringing blackness into view, and her knees gave out from under her.

She never felt Creed's strong arms wrap around her, catching her as she fell.

Chapter Seventeen

Aeryn stumbled through the woods, his head pounding and gasping for air with every breath. He hurt all over. Biting his lip against the pain he pushed harder. His legs screamed in protest, he'd been running for days, sleeping in piles of leaves under trees, under bushes, drinking water from the streams and creeks. Fear gripped him, a feeling just on the edge of panic being his constant companion. His body was about spent. Starvation was slowly eating away at his muscles. If he didn't find the location on the map soon, he knew he would die and part of him almost welcomed death. Death was better than this misery, this constant ache that was soul deep. He pulled the note, crumpled and damp, from his pocket and read it again. It actually wasn't much of a note rather it was just one sentence that meant nothing to him.

The book, the key, Mischa knows.

He stumbled along and his thoughts turned to Mauri and his son. His heart ached with bitter pain; God how he missed them, his world, his family. Tears stung his eyes and snot ran from his nose. He wiped it away with the sleeve of his dirty shirt. He looked down at it and his stomach curled at the odor coming from his body. He was disgustingly filthy.

He couldn't figure out why the guard had set him free. The question churned in his mind. He was a nobody in the grand scheme of things, just another lowlife Gray in their eyes. He wondered who this guard was that he would not only help him but come back to do so. Too many questions with no answers in a situation that made very little sense to him, his head hurt.

He shook his head in frustration, pulled the map from his pocket and once again examined it. Somehow, he'd gotten turned around in the woods; lack of food, rest and dehydration had made his brain foggy. He groaned when he discovered what he'd done. He cleared his mind and corrected his course, set his path and pushed ahead through the terrain taking care to pay attention to the map and his location.

A mere two hours later a small structure came into view. It looked like a small shack. Aeryn bent low behind a large patch of scrub brush and peered through the branches for any sign of movement. Glancing at his map, he calculated his position and questioned if this was the right location. He thought it might be but couldn't be one hundred percent certain. His wary gaze was fixed on the structure he watched. The shack barely stood, crooked and dilapidated, under a grove of heavy spruce. He could see from his hiding spot the two front windows were broken; the door hung askew. It definitely looked abandoned.

Drawing in a deep breath he pushed up from his crouched position and cautiously made his way over the uneven, rocky ground toward the shack. He paused after each couple of steps, his eyes frantic as they searched in every direction for signs of danger.

He reached the front of the shack and peered over the edge of a window but could see nothing. He stepped gingerly onto the porch, carefully avoiding missing boards and rot holes, creaking with each step. He nudged the door with the toe of his boot. A loud screech pierced his ears as it swung open on rusty hinges. He breathed deeply to calm his racing heart and entered the gloomy, shadowed room.

He gasped in surprise as his eyes took in the room. In one corner sat an old desk, the other corner a sleeping pallet on the floor with two folded blankets atop it. Next to the bed was an old potbellied wood stove. In the center of the room stood a wooden table with a plate, cup and spoon on it as if set for a meal. On the wall hung two cupboards, he gazed at the room, its silent tale of whoever had stayed here frozen and covered in dust. Shuffling over to the desk he spied a leather-bound book and on top of it was an old skeleton key. He looked at both in confusion. He reached out and caressed the leather with the tips of his fingers. Books had been banned a long time ago for those without the social score to be deemed worthy of them.

Hunger drove him to open the cupboard doors even though he was sure there was nothing in them. He was surprised when he saw two cans of beans, a container of real coffee and a few biscuits of hardtack neatly wrapped in plastic. He reached in and pulled them down and searched for a can opener or knife to open the beans. His stomach growled painfully. Shuffling through the empty space, he found a knife tucked high upon the cupboard shelf. He didn't know if it was excitement or starvation, but his hands shook as he opened the can. He didn't bother to dump the contents onto the plate; he stood right where he was and just tipped the can to his mouth. He chewed it fast, swallowing one mouthful after another in a desperate attempt to satisfy his hunger.

Once he'd downed the can of beans, he stood holding it in his hand staring across the room. Fatigue left him shaking with weakness. He tossed the empty can onto the floor and made his way over to the pallet and collapsed to his knees on it.

"The book will wait and so can the key," he said aloud. "Right now I just need to sleep."

He fell onto the pallet and the darkness closed in.

Kael

The van slammed against the bumps in the road, each time jarring Kael's body, making him cringe in pain. His hands were snugged tightly behind his back enclosed with metal handcuffs that bit painfully into his wrists. Across from him on a bench seat, sat two guards, men he didn't know, didn't care to know. By the expressions of disdain on their faces, Kael anticipated more beatings from them. So far, they'd kept their slaps and punches to a minimum but he could feel their hatred toward him building.

In their eyes, he was nothing but an animal. Distasteful cargo they were forced into this confined space with. The lowest job they could be assigned as they delivered him to the arena prison.

With a weary sigh of acceptance, he hung his head low and stared at his worn and tattered boots. He wondered what weapon he would be given for his competition in the arena. He hoped for a staff, he much preferred the sleek feel of a simple weapon, its long straight body extending the reach of those who wield it. The simple wooden pole was capable of great assaults as well as defense. It was what he'd trained with. Even having that small advantage could make the difference between life and death for him. He was under no illusions. He suspected he was more than likely going to die. The thought of winning and gaining freedom was too far out of reach for him to even hope for and little more than a distraction. He smiled bitterly. Keifer was dead, that at least gave him a glimmer of satisfaction.

The sudden stop of the van threw Kael onto the steel floor, causing him to yelp in pain. He lay face down unable to right himself, the laughter from the two guards mocking him. One reached down and grabbed him by the hair, hauling him back up.

"I guess this is where you get off!" the guard growled and dragged Kael from the back of the van.

Outside he threw him roughly onto the tar road. A warm trickle of blood tickled its way down to the waistband of his pants and set a chill deep in his heart. The stitches in his back had torn and the wounds began to bleed. He glared up at the guard unable to conceal the hatred in his eyes. He felt numb as he stared at him, the world around him feeling unreal.

"To your feet lowlife," one guard growled menacingly, grabbing him by the back of his neck and hauling him up.

He moaned as he willed his shaky legs to hold him steady.

"March!" the guard hissed, his foul breath wafting toward Kael's nose.

The walls of the arena stood large and looming before him. Two stone arched entry ways that lead him to his death mocked him. He cast his eyes away. He could hear chants and jeers from the crowd lining the street to the prison, exciting themselves into a frenzy for tomorrow's competition. And these people, these so-called humans called him and the Grays animals. He shook his head in disgust. His blood, his competitor's blood, would satiate them. And they would drink of it like fine champagne. Glancing on either side, he gazed into the faces of the crowd as he was led to the arena prison, shackled like an animal, ready for sacrifice. He saw excitement, delight and a few expressions of sadness.

The prison doors in the arena were made of thick, dark steel. The sound echoed when one of the guards rapped his knuckles sharply against it. Kael gasped as he watched it open and the dank smell hit his face. Before him stood a monster of a man, his lips twisted into a grin so cold that terror flooded Kael's heart.

"Here's the prisoner Marco, he's all yours," the guard said.

"Welcome home, Kael," Marco said.

His booming voice shook Kael. He reached out with one massive hand and grabbed him by his shoulder, tossing him into the jaws of the dark hallway. Kael felt weak, terror consuming him as the large steel door shut with a resounding bang.

He was led down the hall, shoved roughly from one side to the other. Marco's hands gripping his shoulder, felt like steel fingers pushing him down a long, dark hallway. Dampness from the stone floor seeped through his worn boots, the smell of decay, rot and human excrement assaulted his nose, making him gag. Single lamps lined the walls every few feet, dripping weak yellow light. Not much, just enough to cast away the darkness.

Kael was yanked to a stop in front of a barred door. The clanking of keys behind him rang in his ears and sent a shiver down his spine. Marco unlocked the cell door with his meaty fist clutched around the set of heavy iron keys and snickered. A rough shove made Kael stumble as his legs struggled to keep up from the force that propelled him forward into a small four by four box. He grunted in pain when Marco drove his fist into his back just below his kidneys.

"Just a little love tap my boy, we'll get really warmed up a little later," Marco quipped as he locked the cell door behind him.

Kael's mind snapped as he sunk to the floor. He stared numbly into the darkness, sitting in a puddle of what he hoped was water but suspected wasn't. He really didn't want to know what it was. The squeak of a rat off to his left caught his attention momentarily. He scoffed at the small creature and laughed inwardly. "In better days, I'd have you for dinner and now you are the one free while I am condemned."

With a deep sigh Kael let his mind drift. Hunger gnawed at his stomach, thirst parched his throat and pain flowed through his body. He could sense the end of all hope. The hope that he once may have had; any hope of surviving this was quickly dissolving into the quagmire of an endless dark abyss.

He remembered a quote his father once said. It was from so long ago, by an author that had long been forgotten, "If you stare into the abyss too long, the abyss stares back into you."

He'd met that darkness and they were now good friends. With a cry of desperation, Kael lay on the cold floor and closed his eyes.

Bacchus

Bacchus had two main objectives. The first was to kill Marco. The other was to bring closure to the subject of Kael. He reached into the cupboard over his kitchen sink and retrieved a small vile of golden liquid. He tucked it safely into a small, hidden pocket on the inside lining of his jacket. With a gleeful whistle, he sat on the blue faux leather sofa and slid on a pair of old army boots. The toe of each boot had been expertly fitted with switch blades; two very sharp blades that would pop out with just a tap of his heel. They were built in so beautifully that even with his keen eyes, he couldn't see the difference between his boots and any others. He stood and bounced on his feet a few times, grinning in approval and familiarizing himself with the feel and snug fit of these boots. He tried to remember the last time he'd worn them and nodded to himself as an image crossed his mind. He'd been good at his tasks and even enjoyed them sometimes. He stretched his aching back and made his way to the front door. He had a few prisoners he needed to visit. With a smile, he gazed up into the bright sunshine as he whistled a merry tune.

He gained entrance to the prison easily enough. It was just a matter of flashing his credentials and growling at just the right pitch. He walked down the dank hallway stopping in front of Calix's cell. With a nod to the guard, he was in. The man slid a key into the keyhole and unlocked the door.

"You can leave us now," Bacchus muttered, not giving the guard a second glance. He stepped into the small cell and waited for his eyes to adjust to the dimness. He saw the man sitting in the corner with his back to the wall and his knees drawn up to his chest, head resting on his knees.

He spoke softly. "Calix, I am from the church. I assume you would like last rites before your competition tomorrow?" he asked.

Pretending to be a priest was easy. He heard a snicker of bitter laughter echo in the small cell.

"Last rites? Who says I'm gonna be the one dying tomorrow?" Calix replied, lifting his head.

Bacchus stared unabashedly into the prisoner's eyes. "I can't force you to accept my offer of prayer son, but I can offer you God's comfort in this time of peril."

He took a step closer and with a motion from his hand so quick it was almost invisible, he pulled the vial of amber golden liquid from his pocket and popped the rubber stopper on the top, careful to not spill a drop of it on his own fingers. He stopped and stood by Calix's water bucket, nothing more than a tin pail with stale and rancid water. He paused and looked at the young man, smiled, and tipped the vile so that only a few drops spilled into it. All the while talking of God to a man who would be dead by this time tomorrow.

"I don't believe in your God, so take it somewhere else Father," Calix sneered bitterly, blithely unaware of the sleight of hand Bacchus had just performed.

"Have it your way son," Bacchus cooed at him kindly. Turning away, but not before he made the sign of the cross, he dipped his head in service and exited the cell.

Once outside the door, he smiled coldly. The toxin he gave Calix would work slowly and by tomorrow's competition; Calix should be unable to cause much harm to Kael. His limbs would be too weak and numb, his vision blurred and his coordination sloppy. With a jaunt to his step he continued down the long dark hallway to Kael's cell.

He was met at the door by Marco. "What are you doing here, Bacchus," the prison warden growled.

Bacchus smiled coldly before answering. He knew that although Marco thought he was king shit on this small hill, he was to Bacchus nothing more than a small irritation. "I've got orders to check on the prisoner Kael, there are those concerned about his welfare," he replied, his voice dripping with silky disgust.

Marco's face blanched with anger. "What are you inferring here, Bacchus? That I abuse the prisoners?" Marco growled.

Bacchus laughed softly, the sound dangerous. "Nope, just that there are those with interest in the young lad in there and I'd hate to see anything, I mean anything happen to him," Bacchus replied, the heavy threat in his voice obvious.

Marco's eyes narrowed. "Nothing will happen to the lad, I'll treat him with kid gloves," Marco spat.

Bacchus nodded. Marco had gotten the message loud and clear. Tonight, Kael could rest without fear of harm. With a grin, he nodded his head toward Marco who stood seething in anger.

"See that you do, Marco," Bacchus quipped.

Spinning on his heels, he made his way back to the entrance door, laughing softly under his breath.

Chapter Eighteen

Zyla sat cross legged on the grass, the sunshine warming her skin. She watched Mischa pack her hand sewn satchel. Tears stood in her eyes, her heart filled with confusion and fear.

"Why are you leaving me?" Zyla asked, her voice cracking with pain.

"Because I have to, you are here for a purpose Zyla. I am no longer needed. They," Mischa replied, waving her arm toward the village, "will take care of you."

Zyla shook her head. "I don't know these people!" She exclaimed. "I don't want to stay here with them! I want to go find Kael, and stay with you, Mauri and Bevin." She cried, tears flowing freely down her cheeks.

"I've explained it to you. Grandfather explained it to you," Mischa snapped in exasperation. "You are to train with Creed, to learn to fight!"

"You can't tell me what to do and neither can he," Zyla spat angrily. "I didn't choose any of this and I'm coming with you." She stood to go for her things.

Mischa grabbed her by each arm and faced her. "You think you get to choose? I didn't choose to be born a Gray and neither did you." "You think you get to choose?" she repeated. "I didn't get to choose when my parents died and neither did you. I have no choice now but to go for Kael and the others, and you have no choice now!" Mischa released her arms and turned away, "Grow up Zyla. It's time you started learning how to protect yourself." She huffed and slung her bag over her shoulder.

Mischa walked away not looking back. It hurt to be so harsh with her, but she needed it. She hoped she would forgive her but no matter what, she needed to learn and learn fast. Tears streamed leaving streaks down Zyla's face. She stood watching Mischa walk away; she'd never been so harsh with her. She was heartbroken and hung her head and cried. Zyla slumped to the ground and thought of the man everyone called grandfather. How much he resembled her mother in looks and mannerisms. Although he was kind enough, she felt that he was also hiding something from her. She could sense it in his tone and his body language. Divulging bits and pieces but never enough for her to put the puzzle together, confusion was her new normal these past weeks.

She was to leave with Creed, to live in hiding up in these very mountains. Creed would train her but she didn't know for what she was training. Training to fight did have a certain appeal after all she'd been through; but no one would tell her why, just that she was to do these things for the betterment of them all.

First, she must be protected as special, and now she must train for the betterment of all; this was all too much for her. She turned her face away, her fingers rubbing at her brow to ward off the first signs of a headache. Over the past few days that she'd been here at the village, she'd gained back more of her strength. It was a wonder what a few days of rest and decent food would do for a body as young as hers. She felt good, better than good, she felt strong. Pressing her lips together, she decided.

They… grandfather and Creed, Mischa and Bevin could decide all they wanted what they thought best for her. But she would have the final say, and she was not staying. If she had to, she'd find her own way back to the village and find out what happened to Kael. With or without their help, she was determined. A pout formed on her lips when images of the journey here flashed in her mind. She'd need to be prepared for the journey ahead.

She pushed herself up from the ground and walked slowly back toward grandfather's shack. Her satchel was there, in the small bedroom she'd spent the last several nights in. She walked head down with purpose and when she glanced up she saw Creed leaning lazily against a post on the porch and grimaced.

"What is with that jerk?" she said

under her breath. "He's nice to everyone but me, what the heck he has against me is a mystery. No matter," she told herself. "I am leaving and good riddance to him." With a sigh, she pushed past him, ignoring his soft laughter.

She'd show him, she wasn't about to stay where she wasn't wanted, and his attitude spoke loudly of him not wanting her here.

It was late into the night when Zyla pushed the window open. When she did, the slight screech of the hinges set her teeth on edge. Mischa had left late that afternoon despite Zyla's begging cries for her to stay. She was now on her own. Holding her breath, she slithered through the partially opened window. Hoisting herself to the hips and sliding through headfirst, she thumped to the ground. The occupants all fast asleep, she prayed they stayed that way. To her it sounded like she'd crashed through the house and out the window with abandon. Although she knew she hadn't, she sat silent at the base of the window listening with wide eyes. After a moment, she got to her feet and looked up at the night sky. She gazed wistfully at the millions upon millions of stars shimmering, twinkling in beautiful synchronicity that mesmerized her. She shook off the moment, quickly brushed herself off and grabbed her satchel. She paused to look up again and after finding the tail of the big dipper she ran in the direction it pointed. She didn't know the difference between north, south east or west, but she did know how to read the stars. The tail end of the big dipper was directly over top Rysa this time of year. All she had to do was keep it in front of her.

Breathing deeply, she inhaled the cool night air into her lungs. The smell of fresh air amazed her. Rysa had a smell, more like a stench, of filth; of a rotting society on the edge of despair. She wrinkled her nose at the thought of going back, but she had to… She had to find Kael.

A bright moon filtered light through the trees and cast a pale glow on the ground in front of her. She picked her way carefully around debris, her ears tuned in and listening to the night sounds. Her mind wandered in the silent freedom of the forest. She had no idea if Kael was alive and ok or if he was still locked away in the garrison prison. She was determined to find him and save him as he'd saved her. A loud but familiar screech echoed through the trees and she knew her wild friend was watching over her. With the false bravado of her youth, Zyla marched toward Rysa.

Creed

Creed slipped silently into the night, the darkness cloaking him. He moved like a ghost, silent, unseen. He kept his eyes trained on Zyla, watching the way her hips swayed and her shoulders rolled as she followed a path that was nothing short of pure instinct. He grinned as darkness enveloped him and his senses followed the age old wisdom of them. The night became alive surrounding him, he drank deeply of it. The shadows danced in the moonlight with the earthy smell of the fresh rain on the floor of the forest. His senses sparked, on fire as he brushed his hand across a rough tree trunk or jagged rock; the sensation lighting up the palms of his hands. He could hear the small cracks of branches beneath her feet and the occasional flap of wings as that ever-present Hawk kept a watchful eye. She was the one. He knew it the moment his eyes met hers. He knew she felt it too, but her inexperience and her youth kept her from seeing what he saw. He growled softly. She would soon see. It was his job to make sure she did. He didn't know why the elders assigned him to her. Her very scent set him on edge; the way she moved sent electricity through his veins but her annoying independence and daring yet meek demeanor made him crazy… or not. She made him feel conflicted. He would do as he was told but he questioned if they could see the effect she had on him.

He suspected she was headed back to

Rysa and watched her curiously. These woods contained far worse than him and he knew she was oblivious to the dangers around her. An owl off in the distance gave a lonesome call and Creed smiled. The hunters were on the prowl and they were hungry. He drew his knife from its sheath on his side and held it at the ready as he followed Zyla. His eyesight in the dark was almost as good as it was in the daylight. He stalked the night, watching and listening, protecting her and lethal to anyone or anything that would try and harm the girl.

"Zyla you little fool," he muttered under his breath with a chuckle.

Part of him drew delight in her bravery. To him, although her bravery was foolish, unrestrained and reckless, it showed him that one day she would make a great warrior and the thought excited him. He just needed to train her into tempering her impulsiveness.

Creed heard the man before he saw him. It was one of the others; a group of nomads who roamed these mountains looking for unsuspecting travelers to rob. They had no honor and cared not for the harm they caused. They were a wild and ruthless people with no ties or loyalties unless it served the moment. He sat perched on a low hanging branch just above where Zyla paused for a rest. He watched as the man slinked his way closer to her, his hands and feet clinging to the tree, he climbed down closer and closer. He was silent and could be deadly unless… that was the worst and Zyla would have to learn this lesson. She didn't even know it but her first lesson began tonight. Holding his breath, Creed watched to see if Zyla would sense the danger. He wouldn't let the man get too close before dispatching him but curiosity held him at bay for the moment.

He watched her and the man in this uncertain dance; her shoulders tensed and her body stiffened; the man held fast. He knew she sensed the danger, but her actions didn't reflect it. His hand gripped his knife, ready to intervene. He watched her as she froze and could almost see the soft rise and fall of her chest with each nervous breath. He muttered under his breath.

"Damn it Zyla, move!" His eyes never wavered for a moment, staring directly at her. His legs tensed and his knees bent, as a cat ready to spring into action. He watched her slightest movements, her eyes narrowed, her jaw tightened; she knew that danger loomed, yet stood frozen. The man was a mere two feet above her, his eyes boring into her. If that man grabbed her, as small as she was, it would be over in a matter of seconds.

"Why isn't she moving? What the hell is she waiting for?" He swore softly, more on a breath than a whisper.

In a flash the man jumped toward her.

He watched in amazement as Zyla just as quickly, rolled to the side, coming up on all fours. She held the position poised for the next move and bore her teeth in a savage grin facing her opponent. In her hand she clasped a rock the size of her fist. Her eyes lit with ferocity. From above, her screeching companion swooped down, it's talons slashing the man's neck and shoulder from behind. He lurched forward to escape the aerial assault just as Zyla threw the rock striking him in his left brow. She reached down and grasped another rock ready to continue her assault. The man reached for his head swiping away the blood from his brow that had begun to trickle into his eye, howling in rage he stomped at her, great puffs of air escaping his flared nostrils with each step.

A valiant effort but she would be no match for this brute. Creed moved like lightening, his knife already in a down swing driving it into the man's thigh. The screams split the night as he swung around and lashed out with his fists. Zyla rolled and dove for the ground. She scrambled backwards as the brawl between he men continued, trying to get away from the fray. Creed withdrew his knife from the man's thigh and plunged it again into his chest. He forced the knife deeper into his ribs until he watched the life leave his eyes. He released the man and his body slumped in a heap onto the ground.

He turned and bared his teeth at Zyla. "You foolish girl!" he roared.

Zyla's eyes widened and filled with anger. "You followed me?" she screamed as she stormed toward him, the rock still firmly set in her fist.

Creed stood up, his eyes challenging her to throw the first swing. Let the lessons begin he thought angrily.

"I followed you!" he growled dodging the small fist that lashed out toward his face.

He easily sidestepped the blow and tapped her hard with one of his own. She gasped as she staggered backward, bringing her hand to her lip where he slapped her. Her eyes filled with fire and she roared in rage launching herself at him. Her assault was all claws and swinging fists; kicks and grunts as she pummeled him. He stood unaffected, taking blow after blow from her, letting her wear herself out. When he saw she couldn't lift her arms anymore, her angry energy was spent. She stepped back and glared at him. He drew a deep breath and swung at her hard, drawing it at the last minute, but still hitting her hard enough to knock her down.

"Don't throw down unless you know you can win," he growled coldly.

He bent and reached a hand down to help her up and laughed when she swatted it away. What this little spitting match showed him was exactly what he wanted to know. Zyla had a temper; she had passion, but she was also clumsy and let her emotions lead her. She could hit hard but had no control over her blows; her movements were wild and uncoordinated fueled by rage and pure anger. What he also saw was determination, courage and a fire that could only come from years of being beaten down and having the guts enough to pull herself back up again and again.

He could work with that...

Chapter Nineteen

Aeryn sat on the front porch of the shack. The roof had long ago caved in, and boards in places were broken and missing. The woods, stood silent around him other than the tweeting of a few birds and the rustling of low ground critters. His eyes burned from the bright sunshine that glared off of the page in the book he was reading. It was difficult for him to sound out some of the larger words because Grays were not allowed to read. His mother taught him bits and pieces as he grew with sticks in the sand, but he'd never read an actual book. For the most part, he understood most of the words, although some of the sentences were difficult to put together. A note he'd found tucked in between the two front pages of the book sat on the porch beside him and every so often he glanced down at it. It all made sense now. Why the social score depended on some rules for the lower classes such as banning books and then eventually banning reading of any kind. This book explained why they'd banned education for anyone below Crimson status. What was taught in their charter schools, before they were outlawed for the Grays, consisted only of mistruths and pretty lies disguised as what they claimed was good for all. But what he was seeing was that it was good for the higher classes. The book held the truth of what the country once was. "Equality for one and all," was written in bold letters, begging his eyes to believe it.

On the very first page, in a fancy script he'd never seen before the title was scribed.

The Constitution of the United States

He picked up the note and sighed, wondering who wrote it. He turned it over in his hands and looked at the paper. It too was thin, soft and white; like nothing he'd seen before this small book. It was meant for him to find. It was meant for someone like him to pick up, and complete the quest presented before him.

He shook his head and bowed it praying he would be strong enough to do what he knew must be done. He opened the note and read the carefully printed words.

"The key, unlock the door and bring the heart to life."

On the bottom of the slip of paper was a map that leads deep into the badlands. It was a frightening place where no sane man dares to tread. He chuckled bitterly as he rubbed his hand against the three-day old stubble that covered his jaw and cheeks.

"Well, I've never been known for being a sane man," he mumbled then chuckled again.

He stood up and slid the note back between the pages of the book and tucked it into his back pocket. Wiping a bead of sweat from his brow he sent up a silent plea.

"Mauri, please forgive me my love, but I have to do this," he said.

Leaving her to raise their son alone shattered his heart. He wished he'd never stolen that food and even that he'd never helped that boy Kael in the prison. He wished he was still in Rysa with his wife and son. Even though they were hungry, they were together. He cringed at the thought of what she might have to do to feed their child and shivered. Wiping a tear from his eye, he stepped off the porch and took the first steps of a journey that would carry him far away.

Zyla

Zyla sat by the fire, trying to drive the early morning chill from her body. She clenched her teeth to keep them from chattering. The night gave her a chance to think and this morning she felt as though she were running uphill against a raging tide. Creed had informed her that she was not going back to Rysa, even if it meant tying her up every single night while he slept. He'd called her everything from a spoilt little brat to a hot-tempered bitch. She listened, he lectured. When she tried to explain, to defend herself against his verbal lashings, he would just growl and glare. And he told her that they were not going back to the village. He would not let her out of his sight for one moment.

Angrily, in the weak light of dawn, she pouted. "Why are you being so mean to me?" she screamed.

"Because you're such a disappointment! I thought you were different. Stronger! But you're not. You are weak and drowning in self-pity. You have done nothing but whine and bitch, complain and pout since Mischa brought you to the village" he snarled.

Zyla stepped back, her eyes wide with hurt. Turning, she glanced away from him to hide her tears, but he was right. Going to Rysa was a foolish idea. She would be arrested the moment she stepped back into that village. She didn't even know if she could trust these people. These Keepers of the Light were strange. It was uncomfortable that they knew her but she didn't know anything about them. All she wanted was to help Kael, but she couldn't do it on her own. She couldn't even get away from these people.

She sighed tiredly and glanced at him. Her heart gave a strange tug that she shook off and ignored. He was handsome, in a rugged, wild sort of way. She let her eyes roam across his face. She admired the strong jaw, the curve of his lips, the high cheekbones that spoke of his Indian bloodlines. Her eyebrows scrunched low over her eyes and she shook her head and growled low in her throat.

He may be nice to look at, but he was anything but nice to her. In fact, she thought him an arrogant bully. Unimpressed she pushed herself up off the ground and stretched her back. A twinge of pain crawled through her spine from the damp chill of the ground. She watched as he gazed at her, brazenly. Her face heated flushing; she turned away.

"So, I'm your prisoner now?" she spat.

He laughed with a husky sound that sent shivers right down to her toes. "Kinda looks that way," he replied, getting up from his sprawled position and feeding another stick into the campfire.

She rolled her shoulders, feeling the pull of the muscles as they stretched. "You don't understand, I need to help my brother, he's all I've got left in this world," she moaned, imploring him to help her.

He sighed, his voice softer. "I can't help you Zyla, I can't save your brother, and neither can you." Reeling in his urge to comfort her he spat, "Look at you," he muttered disgustedly. "What can you, little Zyla, do for him?"

"I could, maybe," she began.

He cut her off. "Can you take on the army of the garrison? Can you pull back a bow and shoot an arrow? Can you fight?"

"I…" she objected.

" No! You're as helpless as a newborn kitten! Going back not only endangers yourself and others who will try to help you; but you are also not helping him!" He snapped at her, with each word stepping closer and closer to her until his face was almost touching hers.

"I can try! I can try!" she screamed,

rage rising up within her.

She was angry but mostly at herself because everything Creed just yelled at her was true. She couldn't fight, she didn't know how; she couldn't shoot a bow or take on an army. Sobbing, she turned away from his hateful glare, a feeling of helplessness washing through her.

Without turning back to him her head hung looking at the forest floor. "Can you teach me these things? Can you?"

Creed scoffed at her even though this is exactly what he'd hoped.

She turned back to him, the tears had streaked lines down her dirt covered cheeks. "Please, help me? I'll work hard to learn Creed," she said, desperation edging her voice.

A grimace curled his lips. "I can Zyla, but not today and not tomorrow, it will take time, right now you have to understand, your brother's fate is in another's hands now," he replied.

She looked down, "I know."

"If we do this, then you are my fate, my purpose. I won't be easy on you; I won't bend if you cry. I may hurt you in order to teach you what you will need to learn," he said, his eyes flashing. "So tell me right now Zyla, is this really what you want?" he hissed.

Zyla bit her lower lip and nodded. Could she be a warrior? Could she become the fighter he said she could? She turned her eyes to Creed's "And will this save my brother?" she asked, "If I learn this?"

Creed shrugged his shoulders. He wouldn't lie to her. "I don't know about your brother, but I know once I'm done, you'll be able to fight and defend yourself. You'll no longer have to cower because you'll be strong, fast. You'll learn to move like a ghost, fight like a warrior, and live purely off the land. This is what I'll teach you," he replied, his eyes cutting into hers. "Are you sure?" He questioned.

She nodded. "I'm sure," she muttered.

He smiled and nodded. This was the Zyla he'd watched from afar. This was the power he'd seen when he first gazed into her eyes.

"Be careful what you wish for, Zyla," he said as he turned to go.

Somehow this felt more threatening to her than anything she'd ever suffered at the hands of the Honor Guard. A chill ran down her spine as she gazed at him.

Deception

Chapter Twenty

Bevin moved quickly through the streets of the city. The early morning light spilled in shadows behind him, elongating his form. The arena was set up, the masses already lining up outside its arched doors waiting for the frenzy of bloodshed. He was in full uniform, so no-one questioned his presence. As a matter of fact, hollow faces stared blankly at him as he passed, they regarded him as little more than a street sign. He may have been the Honor Guard but to them he was barely more than a Gray, just another servant; just one who ate better.

The plan had been set. He was to get in, watch, wait and then spirit Kael away. It sounded simple enough so why did he have a foreboding knot in the pit of his stomach. Shaking it off, he grit his teeth against the urge to lash out at all the apathetic eyes watching his movements. He could never understand how people could enjoy such a barbaric display of violence. Not only did they condone it but turned into a frenzied blood thirsty mob. They should all be mortified, appalled, but instead the public was excited, dancing and shifting around like it was the party of the year and they were invited. It made him sick with disgust.

He'd visited Kael last night in his cell. The boy had all but given up. The slump of his shoulders and haunted shadow in his eyes told Bevin that he was ready to die. He was filthy, battered and desperate. Bevin could offer him no solace, no kind words of encouragement or inspiration.

The fact was Kael would die. But, fate had it only a temporary situation. The plan had to work or that would be his fate. God, he hoped Bacchus knew what he was doing. One mistake and they would not be able to save Kael. Just one and he'd be dead.

The heavy iron door to the prison opened before him by some unknown guard with a pimply face that reminded him of the old saying, pizza face. A thing he'd heard as a youth from the training yard bullies but never did understand. The guy peered past him with shifting, nervous eyes looking at the crowd before he motioned Bevin into the dim interior hallway. Bevin grimaced because he knew what the guard feared the most, vigilante justice. The crowd taking notice and storming the prison, taking it upon themselves to tear Kael limb from limb. He was after all a murderer. He'd killed Akakin with his bare hands. He was guilty. There was no trial, no court, judge or jury, only the word of the guard. And now he was believed to be a monster by public opinion. In this city, public opinion was everything.

The hallway that lead to the arena seating was damp, dark, and moldy smelling.

Iron casters held greasy, soot covered oil lamps adding shadow and mystery to the ambiance. This was considered a particularly useful aspect because it built up the expectations of the fear participants felt. Building on the suspense in anticipation of the bloodletting as the masses traveled through, whispering in hushed excited tones. He on the other hand only felt sadness and desperation, hopelessness and dread. He could imagine this is how the contestants felt as they were led in chains down through this very same hallway when it was time to die.

The arch door opened up to a wide circular arena. Inside, the stands were already starting to fill up in a special seated section just for those with the highest of social scores. They were the elites as most called them even though it was forbidden to do so. He spied Baylin sitting perched excitedly atop her seat in the very first row. Her purple bonnet with matching shawl loosely draped over her shoulders. His eyes caught Asha sitting several seats over, off on the left of Baylin. Her expression in contrast to Baylin was one of disgust and anxiety. The two most powerful women in the city, casting glances at each other. How different they were. Asha was blonde and lithe, demure and known for her kindness. Baylin, dark and exotic, but with a cruel twist to her lips that even a smile couldn't quite erase. It seemed impossible that they, once, had been best friends. Growing up together in a time of turmoil after the war that was now many years past, even they never knew the old world. The years had strained their relationship and now they were cordial but cold. Bevin didn't know what happened to drive such a rift between the two, he never asked and his friendship with Asha never propelled her to tell him why.

He took his seat with the Honor Guard, his rank of Captain gave him a front row view of what would soon be taking place below in the arena, a seat of honor and prominence. He was after all representing the village of Rysa and his garrison who'd captured such a fiend. There was no honor he thought in attending this function, but propriety demanded he must. With nervous energy he took his seat and cast a glance at his fellow guardsmen. From the expressions he saw, not many were happy about having to witness this travesty. Even though Kael had killed Akakin, they all knew what happened. They knew that it was Akakin who'd broken the law and had tried to rape his little sister. Many with sisters, female friends and family quietly whispered that they'd have done the same and admired Kael for his bravery. With a sigh, he settled back against the bench seat and waited. It was almost over.

Bacchus

Bacchus paid one last visit to the prison, avoiding the guard Marco. It was a different guard that led him to the weapons room after his request to see in advance what the contestants would be battling with. The guard opened the door and pointed out the selection made by Kael. Only one got to choose the weapons and the draw had favored him. He chose the staff. Long wooden poles with blades affixed to each end.

He thought about Mischa as he blessed the weapons and placed his poison on each. She was in place and ready to help him in getting Kael out of there once the competition came to an end. She waited deep in the bowels of the prison's secret passageways. He hoped she was ready to face what was ahead. If they were caught their lives would be over. There have only been a few times in the past when women had been chosen to fight in the arena. It was mostly considered a man's world. Bacchus could see that in the event of getting caught, they might put Mischa into the arena and hold a special event as an example. Before he'd let that happen, he'd kill her swiftly and painlessly himself.

He was finished and turned, calling out to the guard. "Where's Marco this fine morning?" he enquired jovially.

The guard, an older man with liver spots lining his face, shrugged his shoulders. "Most likely giving one last pep talk to the contestants," he replied in a gravelly voice.

Marco's pep talks generally involved fists and often times the barbed leather strap used to start the bleeding for the crowds to get them excited when the contestants exited the barred doors leading into the arena.

"Okay then, I guess I shall have to wait until later, after the competition to talk with him," Bacchus lied.

"Humpf," the guard grunted without looking at him.

He had one last job to do. He had to kill Marco. With a smile, he waved dismissively to the guard and made his way out of the weapons room, walking down the hall leading back toward the arena. He glanced over his shoulder at him; he'd gone back to his position of leaning against the wall.

He darted to the left and stepped off into a side corridor unseen by the guard. Bacchus made his way toward Marco. He knew exactly where he was and winced when he heard Calix's screams from behind his cell door. Marco's gift to the prisoners was one last beating before the competition. He shook his head in disgust and knocked on the cell door interrupting him

"What?!" Marco roared from behind the door.

"It's me, Bacchus. Step out here immediately!" Bacchus commanded.

There was a muttered curse then another body blow followed by a howl of pain before an angry Marco opened the door and stormed out. "What do you want?" Marco growled, his face flushed from his ministrations.

"I have orders to bring you to see Baylin. She wants to discuss something with you," Bacchus lied, his stomach curling in disgust as he glanced at the slime of blood on Marco's meaty hands.

"Now?" Marco asked, his tone changing from one of anger to one of curiosity.

Bacchus smiled coldly and nodded. "Yes, she says it's important that she talk with you before the competition," Bacchus replied.

Marco sighed and wiped his hands. He actually liked this part of his job and tried to hide his disappointment at being called away. "Okay, take me to her," he replied. He'd come back and finish with Calix later.

Bacchus led Marco down the long, dimly lit hallway toward the back of the prison. He heard the man behind him mutter about all the secrecy and how he couldn't understand why Baylin couldn't have met him in his office. Bacchus ignored it and kept leading him deeper and deeper into the darkest parts of the prison.

When they reached a room with a locked door, Bacchus turned and smiled. "Go ahead in, she is waiting for you," he said pleasantly.

Marco huffed as he stepped passed him into the dark room after Bacchus made a show of unlocking the door. As he walked past, Bacchus palmed his knife and stepped in behind him.

"Okay, so, where is she?" Marco growled, turning toward Bacchus. His eyes widened in terror as he saw the cold gleam in Bacchus's eyes.

"Asha told me to give you this," Bacchus replied as he drove his knife deep into Marco's chest, puncturing his heart. He stared into Marco's eyes as horror, astonishment, surprise and finally death flitted across them. Stepping away, he released him and let the man's body fall to the floor in a crumpled heap. Swiftly, he wiped the blade of his bloody knife onto Marco's shirt, cleaning it off.

"May your evil soul rot in hell, Marco," he spat at the corpse on the floor. He stepped out the door and locked it behind him before he made his way back toward the arena. "It'll be a long while before anyone finds you," he grinned.

Kael

Kael moved awkwardly. His feet and

hands bound by shackles. The guards lead him down the dark, dank hallway toward the arena. They pushed, shoved, kicked and spat on him as he walked. His mind grew fuzzier with each step he took toward his death, his heart accepting this as his fate. Pain coursed through every muscle, every tendon that had been stretched too far and every bone that had felt the blows of these past two weeks. A thin ray of sunlight spilled through a crack in the arched doorway. Something so pleasing in this dark place only carried an omen of what was to come. The arena was packed by now with spectators hungry for his blood. He gasped when he saw none other than Calix, bound in a similar manner already standing and waiting at the entrance door.

"Calix?" he whispered to his friend.

Calix turned his battered face toward him. He was shocked by the hatred pouring from his eyes. "You!" Calix hissed with a cold grin from his split and bloody lips. "It was supposed to be you all along, not me!" Calix growled.

Shuffling a step back, Kael looked at him, his gaze questioning. "What are you saying? Why are you here my friend?" Kael whispered.

Calix's lips curl into a sneer. "Friend?" He hissed, leaning toward him, "you were never my friend!"

Kael squinted his eyes looking at him suspiciously. "You helped save Zyla," he protested.

Calix scoffed, "I'd hoped Akakin took care of you and your sister. I loathed you both!"

"But," Kael protested.

"Baylin paid me to keep an eye on you, paid me to set you up so she could watch you die in the arena!"

Kael's eyes widened. He'd been set up. The thoughts flashed wildly through his mind. He barely even knew who this Baylin was and couldn't figure out why he and Zyla would be set up. He glared at him. Kael spoke softly, "a fitting end for you then."

Calix laughed, "I'm the one who's going to kill you Kael and I will draw out every ounce of pain from you I can before I finish you off!"

Kael felt an anger, a ferocity he'd never felt before surge inside him, coursing through his veins as a red haze descended over his mind. Calix, whom he'd thought of as a friend, whom he'd trusted with both his life and Zyla's was a traitor. He was the one who'd turned Kael in. It was because of him that Zyla was missing and he was here in the arena. He didn't know who in the hell this Baylin was he spoke of but if he lived through this he'd find out. He roared and launched himself at Calix, wanting to rip him to shreds. Laughter echoed from the guards when they pulled him roughly away.

"Save it for the arena boys," one of the guards chuckled.

The doors flung open and sunlight flooded the entry blinding him. One of the guards released his shackles and shoved a staff into his hands. He was roughly pushed out through the door into the sunlight with Calix right behind him. His ears rang with the roar from the crowd as he stumbled into the center of the circle.

With wide eyes he looked around at the crowd while the announcement screamed over the loudspeakers above. He turned in a circle, staff in hand disoriented and stunned. Calix stood frozen across from him and his mind cleared with rage welling up within.

Bevin

Bevin felt the roar of a thousand screams before his ears registered the sounds. They pulsed through his body as he watched Kael and Calix stumble into the arena. Spectators stood, screaming and clapping their hands in excitement, the look on their faces was almost feral. From the corner of his eye he caught sight of Bacchus entering the stands. He glanced at him and gave a slight nod. It was done. Now it was just a matter of time. He sucked in a deep breath and set his gaze on the arena below.

The horror clutched his throat when the first hit sliced deeply into Kael's thigh, blood spattering the dirt. A roar of satisfaction erupted behind him and he heard amidst the noise, one lady scream in pleasure as she shouted out, "First blood!"

Kael fell to one knee and bowed his head as he dropped his staff to the dirt. Bevin muttered under his breath, urging the boy to get up and fight. Calix launched himself at his injured opponent and Bevin's heart was in his throat. Kael rolled onto the ground and back up on one knee grabbing his staff in one motion. With a roar he thrust out at Calix catching him solidly under the chin and sending the stunned Calix to the ground, spitting out a wad of blood.

Bevin shuddered as he watched the battle before him. He cast a glance at Bacchus who stood tall and confident with a small smile forming on his lips.

Kael

His limbs felt heavy as he lifted the staff. His thigh pulsed with pain. His mind, foggy and numb grasped at the question of what was happening to him. He didn't feel right. Something inside of his gut was screaming at him that this numbness, this weakness wasn't right. But he had no time to pay attention to that. Gasping for breath, he twirled away from Calix's next move, the bladed end of his staff barely missing his face.

Kael jumped backward and lost his balance as Calix more staggered than charged toward him. The crowd roared with excitement when Calix brought the blade end of his staff down across his chest, cutting through his shirt leaving a gash deep and long. He felt the gush of blood as it ran down over his stomach. Fiery pain shot through him and his legs gave out again, shrinking to get away from Calix's blows. Thrusting his staff upward it sank into Calix's stomach and he heard the howl of agony burst from Calix's lips, momentarily giving him reprieve. He was sweating; his mind foggy with pain but Kael crawled to his feet and faced Calix. He lashed out with a swift stab of the staff once again drawing blood from his opponent. The crowd went crazy with bloodlust as they chanted words that couldn't penetrate his chaotic mind.

A sharp and intense pain that felt like a razor drove deep into his shoulder dropping him to one knee again. Blood, from both him and Calix, stained the dirt, a painting in red surrounding them. Darkness danced at the edge of his vision and he swung wildly with his staff, blinded by the blood that poured into his eyes from a slice across his forehead. His ears filled with grunts, hisses of pain, howls of agony. He fought desperately against the person he once thought of as his friend. Sparkles danced before his eyes as blow after blow, pummeled his body. His stomach erupted and he vomited onto the ground and his knees gave out. He never felt the last blow as Calix drove the blade end of his staff with his own dying breath into Kael's back right between his shoulder blades.

Bevin

Bevin stood and watched the field medic run into the arena. The man bent, checking Kael first, flashing a look to Bacchus, he raised his hand giving the sign of death. He moved to Calix and did the same. A roar erupted from the crowd, laughter and screams filled the air. Bevin stood, glanced at Bacchus, nodded and made his way out of the stands. The boy had taken a hell of a beating. Blood stained the dirt as two guards lifted Kael's limp body and unceremoniously dragged him back toward the archway door, followed by another two guards doing the same for Calix. Bevin walked slowly toward the morgue where both boys would be taken. It was there that Bacchus would be waiting. Pushing his way through the crowd that had gathered for a glimpse of the bodies, he descended into the dark hallway. The smells of urine, feces, blood and rot were overwhelming and made him gag. He spied Bacchus outside the morgue door.

"You ready?" Bacchus said.

Bevin nodded. "Yeah, let's get this done."

Together they entered the morgue and spied Kael laid out on a steel table. Bacchus bent and place his ear against the boy's chest while Bevin stood watch at the door.

"He's alive, barely, but his heart is still beating."

Bevin nodded. "Okay, then let's get him out'a here," he hissed, nervous that someone would come down the hallway and catch them.

Together they lifted Kael from the table and quickly made their way, half carrying and half dragging his unconscious body deep into the silent and empty hallways toward the back of the prison. Bacchus stopped, his breath rasping in and out, he moved a grate and slid down into a partially flooded tunnel. Reaching up his arms, he caught Kael as Bevin passed the boy down to him.

"Okay, I've got him from here my friend," Bacchus said as he gazed up from the darkness into Bevin's eyes.

Bevin nodded. "God speed my friend," Bevin said and slid the heavy metal grate back into place. He turned and quickly retraced his steps back to the arena. In his haste to leave the area he failed to hear a soft chuckle as one of the guards stood in the shadow's watching him.

He rounded a corner and his heart dropped when he saw a shadowed figure moving fast ahead of him. He watched the figure run up to a pair of guards, turn and point in his direction. Both guards drew their weapons as they advanced on him. Bevin steeled himself.

"This guard says he saw you taking the prisoner's body. Where did you bring it?" one of the guards snarled.

Bevin stood defiantly and glared into the man's eyes. "You'll never find him," he spat.

The other guard grabbed him and spun him around, placing handcuffs on his wrists. "We'll see about that!" the guard growled in his ear.

Bevin smiled. He'd been caught. He'd accept the consequences, but Kael was safe.

Mischa

Mischa bent low over Kael's body on

the dirty floor of the tunnel. She worked quickly, her hands searching out each wound, rinsing it with bottled water and slapping a bandage over it. Kael's breathing was laborious as he struggled for life.

"How much poison did you give him?" she hissed, glaring up at Bacchus.

He shook his head as he pulled a vial, the antidote, from his pocket and spilled two precious drops into Kael's mouth, under his tongue. "Just enough to make his heartbeat slow," he replied.

Her eyes filled with tears as she looked down upon the man she loved, his face ashen. Her heart thudded painfully in her chest and she drew a deep, ragged breath.

"He's lost a lot of blood, he's in shock, I don't know if he'll live Bacchus," she whispered.

"We can only hope he survives, Mischa," Bacchus replied as he watched her gather up her medical supplies and place them back into her carry pack.

Bending, his knees popping off like gunshots, he picked Kael up and slung him over his back in a fireman's carry. Glancing at Mischa he nodded for her to lead the way. They needed to keep moving.

Bevin

He stood before Baylin, his wrists bound by handcuffs. He watched her pace the floor angrily. He'd been brought to an inner chamber, away from the prying eyes and listening ears of others.

"He's alive, isn't he? You can't tell me you'd steal a dead body, so he must be alive!" she hissed.

The gravity of the situation struck her and Bevin stared at her blankly. Neither of them confirming nor denying her accusation.

She twirled on the guard standing at the door. "You," she pointed. "Go find him! You go down into those tunnels and bring Kael back to me along with whoever is helping this traitor!" she screamed, her eyes lit with fury.

The guard nodded. Bevin smiled. They would never find Kael. Not deep in the bowels and passageways that ran beneath the prison and the streets of the city. Under there, a maze of corridors that snaked for miles in endless twists and turns.

He groaned under his breath at the carelessness of being caught. He should've kept a keener eye out for this, but he hadn't thought that any of the guards would have reason to be that far back in the unused portion of the prison.

"You!" Baylin smiled coldly as she growled through gritted teeth, "will pay dearly for your actions!" she threatened.

Her face twisted in fury and her eyes glistened with insanity. Bevin bowed his head. He was sure he would pay, but to him the price was worth it knowing he'd saved Kael.

Asha

Asha bent her head as she listened while the maid whispered in her ear. The girl had been waiting in the servant's chamber along with other servants for the meeting to finish. She whispered, "I just saw two guards march down the hall with Bevin in handcuffs."

Asha listened and her heart thudded with cold fear. "Hold on," she said. And rustled around her purse pulling a pad and pen from it, she hastily wrote a quick note. "Deliver this to the General's driver, Ryder, right now," she ordered.

The girl looked at her with a concerned expression on her face. "Yes ma'am," she replied.

Asha sighed worriedly. She wasn't about to let Baylin arrest Bevin. She'd find a way to help him even if it meant tearing the whole Honor Guard apart. Ryder, the general's driver would get the information to Rysa where it needed to go.

She rose from the bench seat and went in search of her once best friend determined to find answers. She intended to get to the bottom of what Baylin had on him and why he'd been arrested.

Mischa

The long passageway smelled of rot and stagnant water, sickening her as she splashed her way through the last few feet toward the outside. An iron grate was all that barred her from freedom. With all her strength she shoved it, a mighty grunt escaped, and she pushed it outward breathing in the fresh air. The sunshine warmed her face as she stepped out onto the embankment. Bacchus stepped out beside her and turned his face up to the sun. He hated the underground tunnels.

"There will be time later to enjoy the fresh air," he said.

A wave of her arm motioned toward the waiting truck, they hurried over to it and laid Kael onto the truck bed, pushing two piglets away they covered him with hay and rotted, filthy blankets. Indignant squeals felt as if gongs were echoing their location. Bacchus nodded to Mischa, "We should hide you as well. You're wanted."

"Only in Rysa, they wouldn't recognize me here," she said.

Relief flashed across his face realizing she was right; it was a local thing and soon it would be over. He offered a weak smile and climbed onto the passenger seat.

"Okay, drive normally, watch the road and do not stop for anyone," he warned as he drew an old handgun from beneath his jacket.

Only the soldiers were allowed weapons and Mischa raised an eyebrow in surprise as he checked his weapon.

"From my time in the war," he smiled at her.

She nodded and shifted the truck into gear, glancing in the rearview mirror making sure one last time that Kael's body was hidden.

"Okay, let's get you to the Keepers of the Light my love," she whispered to herself.

She drove the truck slowly through the streets of the city. She'd take him to where she knew he'd be safe and to the only people she trusted. With a sigh, she drove steadily; Bacchus beside her, his gun at the ready.

"Bacchus?" she asked as she steered the truck through the crowds leaving the arena.

"Yes?" he replied.

She felt tears sting the back of her eyes.

"Do you think we'll ever win?" she asked.

He shrugged his shoulders. "I don't know Mischa, we can only keep trying," he whispered on a soft sigh.

Another deep sigh escaped him and he wondered if he was getting too old now to lead this fight. One glance at his granddaughter steeled his resolve. She deserved to be free and he would do everything in his power to bring her that freedom.

They had a long journey ahead of them and many would die. He tightened his jaw and stared into the side view mirror, his heart heavy with pain as he watched the city fade from his sight.

ACKNOWLEDGMENTS

Thank you to all the Beta readers and editorial staff, your detailed feedback and critique are necessary for the production of the works.

Thank you, Dave Farris, Rachel Jodoin, Susan Isenberg for your read throughs and comments.

Much gratitude goes out to our editorial staff, Ali Maloney, WMH Cheryl for their repeated passes on each round of developmental and line edits. All of you make our words sparkle and come to life.

To the fans on Facebook in the Written Apocalypse group, you keep us writing.

ABOUT

DJ Cooper

DJ Cooper spends her days writing these dystopian and post-apocalyptic novels. As owner of Prepper Podcast Radio Network her affinity to the preparedness community helps fuel stories that offer insights into ways they too can emerge from these kinds of moments.

"I love to hear from readers! Find books and chat or even learn about preparedness in any of the medias below."

On the web

https://authoroftheapocalypse.com

Social Media

https://facebook.com/authordjcooper

https://twitter.com/djcooper2015

https://instagram.com/author_djcooper

Email Me

Dj.cooper@angryeaglepublishing.com

Find all my books on the

AMAZON AUTHOR PAGE

https://www.amazon.com/DJ-Cooper/e/B01182KS32

ABOUT
N.A. Broadley

N.A. Broadley spends her days writing magical stories and tending her critters on the homestead, hear about her adventures on her podcast Around the Homestead on Prepper Podcast.

"I love chatting with readers and sharing my homestead adventures. My current endeavor is class for herbals. Join the journey and learn with me, chat me up!"

On the web

https://nabroadley.com

Social Media

Facebook.com/NA-Broadley-Author-2315285068538146

https://twitter.com/holisticnancy

Email Me

na.broadley@angryeaglepublishing.com

Find all my books on the

AMAZON AUTHOR PAGE

https://www.amazon.com/N-A-Broadley/e/B07V282K4K

Thank you for reading

Book 2 of

The Insurrection Trilogy

— Evasion —

Coming May 2020